MURDER IN FRANCE

A 1920S COZY HISTORICAL MYSTERY

LEE STRAUSS

Library and Archives Canada Cataloguing in Publication

Title: Murder in France / Lee Strauss.

Names: Strauss, Lee (Novelist), author.

Series: Strauss, Lee (Novelist). Ginger Gold mystery ; 21.

Description: Series statement: A Ginger Gold mystery ; book 21

Identifiers: Canadiana (print) 20220432805 | Canadiana (ebook) 20220432813 | ISBN 9781774092361 (hardcover) | ISBN 9781774092330 (softcover) | ISBN 9781774092347 (IngramSpark softcover) | ISBN 9781774092354 (Kindle) | ISBN 9781774092378 (EPUB) Classification: LCC PS8637.T739 M8775 2022 | DDC C813/.6—dc23

Murder at the Royal Albert Hall

Murder in Belgravia

Murder on Mallowan Court

Murder at the Savoy

Murder at the Circus

Murder at the Boxing Club

Murder in France

Murder at Yuletide

The swimming pool room had been closed for the party. Lady Ginger Gold, now known as Mrs. Basil Reed, had stipulated that festivities would take place on the grounds of Villa Legrand. The mid-September weather was pleasantly warm, but if guests lingered into the evening and became chilled, the fireplace in the grand room would be lit, and the party would move inside.

Ginger had been searching for her restless fifteen-year-old son, Scout, who'd expressed absolute disinterest in "stuffy gatherings of adults, most of whom he could barely understand" and had wandered off. He'd learned to swim during the month the family had been holidaying in France. Some days, it had been so hard to get him out of the pool that by the time he'd climbed out, his skin had shrivelled like damaged leather.

She was surprised to find her dearest friend Haley beside the pool with her long arms folded over her chest. A light breeze lifted a few stray brunette curls off Haley's cheek as she leaned against the wall and stared at the blue water.

Haley flashed half a smile when she spotted Ginger. "I've never learned to swim."

"I perfected the dog paddle in a swimming hole in the Charles River," Ginger said. "It was so cold that the incentive to learn quickly was great."

"The cattle drank out of a pond near our farm," Haley said. "My brothers and I would go in to cool off, but not over our heads. It never got deep enough. Just a lot of mud, really. Our mother would get so angry; she'd make us wash our clothes afterwards." Her wide smile broke into a chuckle. "It was worth it, though."

Ginger's heart softened at the mention of Haley's brothers. It was the murder of her brother Joseph three years earlier that had caused Haley to suddenly leave London for Boston. Sadly, his case remained unsolved.

"Can I entice you to return to the party with me?" Ginger asked gently.

The humidity in the room was sure to make her perfect finger curls grow limp. She was surprised Haley wasn't concerned about the effect on her tremendous collection of natural curls, ready to rise and break free of her faux bob. "Unless you've chosen this evening to learn to swim?"

"I just needed a little quiet," Haley said, taking Ginger's arm. "I'm ready to, once again, face the hordes."

Ginger laughed as she led her friend to the back garden, where the guests ate French desserts, drank local wines and cocktails. "This is hardly a horde," Ginger refuted.

"Ten and as many servants scurrying about," Haley returned.

Ginger conceded that her lifestyle sharply contrasted with that of her American friend, who liked to live alone and in humbler circumstances. But Ginger was delighted and grateful for the luxurious villa, which, for the last month, had proven to be a refuge to the Reed clan, who'd barely escaped the claws of a family nemesis. It was time to rest, relax, and see the sights. And for Ginger, the icing on the cake was that Haley Higgins had come from Boston to work on her medical practicum. Ginger had delighted in every spare minute Haley had taken away from her studies. She would soon be a pathology doctor, and Ginger mused that it would be a quiet profession. When it came to socialising, her friend preferred small numbers, and Ginger appreciated her effort to step out with this vivacious crowd.

Most of those present were Ginger's family: her husband Basil stood by the three-tiered concrete fountain, conversing with the charismatic Earl of Witt. Lord Davenport-Witt, known as Charles to the family, had married Ginger's former sister-in-law Felicia, the sister of Ginger's late husband, Daniel, Lord Gold.

The Dowager Lady Gold was seated in the shade beside her granddaughter Felicia, and Ginger could hear snippets of joyous language regarding their return home to London in the morning.

Ginger had thrown the gathering because her family would return to England the next day without herself and her infant daughter Rosa. Her maid Lizzie and Rosa's nanny would remain behind as well. The other reason for the soirée was that she'd learned of a fashion parade that week and had secured an invitation from one of her guests, Mme Sabine Chapdelaine.

Basil had been reluctant to agree to his wife's delayed return to Hartigan House, but since she ran a Regent Street dress shop, she could hardly miss an opportunity to advance her business. This explained her other guests, Monsieur and Madame Rochefort, and the current queen of Parisian fashion design, and Mme Sabine Chapdelaine's date, M. Bernard. Ginger had also invited Mr. Brian Miller, and his French wife, Mrs. Aurélie Miller, from New York, at Mme Chapdelaine's request.

"Does it not bother you that Mme Chapdelaine's date keeps looking your way?" Haley asked.

The man in question had been introduced to her as M. Roger Bernard. His hair was styled fashionably, a side parting slickly combed to the side, and his attractive face was cleanly shaven. He favoured a leg and Ginger wondered when the injury had occurred. Though they'd met long ago, Ginger was pretending this evening was their first acquaintance. He was putting on a similar act, but not before Ginger had caught the recognition that, for a split second, had flashed behind his eyes.

"You and Mme Chapdelaine share a resemblance," Haley said. The French designer's red hair was styled similarly to Ginger's, in a short bob with rows of finger curls. "Maybe M. Bernard has a preference for redheads."

Ginger kept her expression a blank look of disinterest. "I'm certain Mme Chapdelaine will grow tired of him in no time."

"You're probably right," Haley said. "The French and their passions ignite and extinguish quickly."

"Surely not all," Ginger said with a bubble of laughter.

"I've been in Paris for less than two months, and my fellow student is already on his third *jolie fille*."

"Are you saying there will be no *garçon* for you, Miss Higgins?"

Raising a brow, Haley glanced down at Ginger. "I've no time for such exploits, Mrs. Reed."

Before Ginger could respond, Scout ran across the lawn with Boss, Ginger's black-and-white Boston terrier, racing behind.

"I think Scout might actually miss France when he's back in London," Ginger said as she smoothed her evening gown. Like Mme Chapdelaine, she wore a Jean Patou, more form-fitting than earlier in the decade, yet with the same low waist. The champagne-coloured fabric glistened in the outdoor candlelight, a large matching bow adorning the gown's lower back, and an uneven, handkerchief hemline hung delicately around her calves. Ginger continued, "You should've heard his fuss when he learned he was coming here for a month. He does bring up the horses daily. He'll be happy to return to them. And, of course, he mustn't miss any more school."

Though Ginger was talking about her son, her gaze moved to her fellow redhead, who, standing with Roger Bernard, had been joined by Gaspard Rochefort and Mr. Miller.

"The French were the first to make an industry out of fashion, Brian," Mme Chapdelaine said, surprising Ginger at her familiar use of the man's first name. Her voice had become louder with each drink, and she toppled slightly as she waved her glass-carrying hand in the air, the contents of the glass sloshing back and forth. "We have been exporting our style since the seventeenth century, before most of the world realised what fashion was." With a haughty look, she added, "Including America."

The fashion designer listened raptly to what the gentlemen were saying in return. Their voices remained low and muffled, and Ginger couldn't discern what was said, though she could see that Gaspard Rochefort was speaking.

Mme Chapdelaine's head fell back as she laughed. Placing a dainty hand on M. Rochefort's arm, she trilled, "Rochefort designs are, er, *agréables*."

"She is *une sorcière*."

Ginger jumped at the sound of Mme Rochefort, who had come up from behind. "She's a siren in the sea, calling sailors to their demise. Look at her! I visit the lavatory for ten minutes, and she has her hooks in my husband."

Sabine Chapdelaine had called the Rochefort designs *nice*. Hardly impassioned praise.

"Actually, *he* approached her," Haley clarified.

Ginger tossed her a look that said, mind your own business, American. Haley smirked.

Mme Rochefort fancied make-up and applied it generously, but no amount could hide the deep wrinkles that had formed with age. Her confidence was intact, and she seemed undaunted by Haley's statement. "Phewy. She's jealous of our designs. They are *avant-garde*. Hers are tired and *fin de siècle*."

"I look forward to viewing designs from you both at the show," Ginger said. She locked eyes with a waiter and nodded to the gramophone on the balcony. The record had ended, and only the sounds of the wind through the trees and the engines of motorcars in the city could be heard.

The waiter responded in haste, placing the

needle at the beginning of a new record, but not before M. Rochefort's voice pierced through.

"We shall see who reigns supreme." M Rochefort spun on his heel, sputtering French curses. "Her time will soon come to an end."

After the scratchy intro, American jazz filled the air, diverting everyone from their shock over M Rochefort's outburst. "Everyone, let's dance!" Ginger took one of Basil's hands, and he placed the other on her hip and expertly led her in the foxtrot.

"Madame Reed," he said with a smile, "you are divine. You make it very difficult for me to leave you behind." His hazel eyes sparkled, crow's feet spreading from the corners, and butterflies fluttered in Ginger's stomach when his full lips pulled up. Allowing him to leave without her was not a simple endeavour for her either.

"You'll have a case to keep your attention, I'm sure," she said. "London crime never rests."

"I'm looking forward to going back," Basil said. "One can only eat crusty bread and mature cheese for so long."

Ginger followed Basil's steps in perfect time. They were good dancers.

"I adore the bread and cheese, but I agree it's

time to return home," she said. "If it weren't for the fashion parade, I'd be on my way as well."

M. and Mme Rochefort had joined them on the lawn, along with Charles and Felicia, Mr. and Mrs. Miller, and Mme Chapdelaine and M. Bernard, despite his damaged leg.

Haley had taken Felicia's empty seat and attempted conversation with Ambrosia. Ginger and Basil glided by close enough to hear.

"French food is much too rich," Ambrosia said as she leaned against her walking stick. "And getting a good cup of tea is nearly impossible."

After another turn about the lawn, they were interrupted by M. Bernard. "May I cut in?" he asked. Ginger hesitated before saying, "But what of your partner?"

Roger Bernard inclined his head towards Mme Chapdelaine, who watched them as she waited. "It was her idea. She would be delighted to have a dance with M. Reed, should he oblige."

"Of course," Ginger said, giving her husband a gentle nudge. "I want my guests to feel satisfied."

Ginger smiled at her partner but stayed quiet. A glance at Basil and Mme Chapdelaine proved that she was purring seductively and had no reservations about clinging to another lady's husband in the wife's presence. Good thing Ginger wasn't the jealous type.

"Does that bother you?" M. Bernard asked in French. Before she could answer, he added, "Mademoiselle Baton. Or should I say, LaFleur?"

So, he *had* recognised her. It was the blasted red hair. Even though she'd worn it long and braided for most of the war, it was a liability. Ginger had hoped that the fact she'd had a rounder face when she was younger, and rarely wore make-up in those days, would've helped her to avoid detection. It wasn't like she was the only redheaded lady in the world. There were two present that very evening.

"Louis," Ginger returned, using the name she'd known him by, if only for the briefest of missions. Switching to French, she said, "I suppose one couldn't return to France without the chance of encountering a ghost."

"I admit, your English accent threw me. I honestly believed you were French."

"Then I did my job well."

"You did. And life seems to have rewarded you."

"It has. I'm very happy." Ginger added, "You look good."

He'd put on a few pounds since she'd seen him

and appeared healthy and strong. "Mme Chapdelaine must treat you generously."

M. Bernard chuckled. "I'm in vogue for the week." His hands disappeared into his trouser pockets. "I understand you are staying in Paris after your husband leaves."

"Just for a week." Ginger was tiring of having to defend herself.

"Well, if you lack for company . . ." M. Bernard winked.

The French! She gaped at her dance partner, nearly pushing him aside. "M. Bernard," she said with tight lips. "You're very much changed since the last time we met."

Indeed, as Louis, he had been a broken man with familial losses too terrible to imagine. In those days, he'd been morose and lacking in hope. Certainly not a vessel of joy. Nor had he been in the mood to make romantic advances!

The humour disappeared from his eyes. "The war was a long time ago, Mrs. Reed. Survival demands that one moves on. I meant no offence."

Ginger felt a twinge of regret. How could she be put out that a Frenchman behaved like the rest of his lot? When it came to romance and relationships, the

French had very different opinions and values from the British and Americans.

"Please, M. Bernard," Ginger said, returning to English. The music had stopped between songs. "Would you fetch me a lemonade?" she asked. "I believe I saw a staff member refill the jug." Two maids were delivering drinks to those who'd had their fill of dancing.

"It would be my pleasure, Madame Reed." Ginger watched as the man pivoted on his good foot and limped away to do her bidding.

2

Ginger was pleased to see that the cocktails were made to her guests' satisfaction, despite the absence of the barman. The French loved their cocktails, and the Americans were especially grateful, particularly the Millers, to be free to imbibe without fearing Prohibition agents threatening arrest.

The men tended towards highball drinks like Tom Collins, a gin sour. The ladies requested sweeter and more colourful cocktails with fancy names like the White Lady, the Gin Fizz, and the Sidecar.

As she watched her guests mingle, Ginger sipped a White Lady—a delightful citrusy concoction of gin, lemon juice, and orange liqueur topped with a layer of foamy egg white.

Brian Miller was conversing intensely with Basil about American social issues of concern to him. "They're putting telephone service from the United States to Mexico. Can you imagine that? I can think of plenty of better places the government could put their money."

"I imagine telephone service will reach every country eventually," Basil returned.

"Can't imagine," Mr. Miller said with a shrug. "I still don't understand how sound can move through wires like that."

Basil rubbed his chin. "The world is changing quickly."

Felicia moved in beside Ginger. "It seems like your party is a great success."

"I'm glad everyone is having a good time."

From the corner of her eye, Ginger caught Felicia briefly wince, her hands pressed on the back of her hips.

"Are you all right, Felicia?" Ginger asked with mild concern. Her former sister-in-law was with child but still early in the process. No one would know to look at her.

"My back aches," Felicia said. "Too much time on my feet, I suppose."

"You should sit down." Ginger linked her arm with Felicia and led her to an empty chair.

Sabine Chapdelaine's laughter broke through, and Ginger and Felicia twisted their necks to see what had precipitated the outburst. Mme Chapdelaine held a drink in the air while grabbing on to Charles, who was strolling by. "Don't let me fall, *mon cher*. That's better. Oh, it's you. Why don't we dance?"

"It might be time to close the bar," Felicia said tersely. "Mme Chapdelaine appears to have forgotten who brought her to the party."

Ginger's gaze sought Louis, who stood to the side of his inebriated date, frowning deeply.

Charles, a man of much diplomacy, handled the situation with grace, untangling Mme Chapdelaine's arm from his and ushering her towards Louis. "My dear Bernard," he said, "I do believe this lovely lady is with you."

Ginger noted the smile of appreciation that crossed Felicia's face as Charles made his way back to her.

Basil had joined them, and Ginger asked him to announce that the bar would be closing.

"Then we must all have one more!" Mme Chapdelaine said.

Ginger nodded her approval to Beaufort, who took orders and returned to the bar. The extra staff Ginger had hired had left once the party's dinner had ended, leaving the villa staff to finish up.

Only a few guests requested a final drink, Bérénice Rochefort, and both of the Millers, along with Mme Chapdelaine. At the last minute, Ginger ordered another White Lady. It was her second drink of the evening, and she thought she could use a little help unwinding at night to fall asleep.

Ambrosia meandered over, and Ginger noticed how the dowager leaned more heavily on her walking stick than she used to.

"I think I've had enough of the party, Ginger," she said. "You won't mind if I dismiss myself?"

"Not at all, Grandmother."

The maids and footman scurried about, removing dirty glasses and presenting new pretty drinks. A crystal-cut glass with a blue tint caught Ginger's eyes. The villa glasses were normal crystal with a distinct cut-glass design. Perhaps her guests had gone through the usual glassware, and it was quicker to bring out the blue addition than to wash another glass.

Lizzie approached, and Ginger was about to assign her the task of accompanying Ambrosia to her room, but the maid interrupted. "Nanny Green asked me to seek you out, madam. Little Rosa is teething badly and will not be comforted."

"Grandmother," Ginger said as she lent an arm. "Allow me to walk up the stairs with you."

Basil tapped her elbow. "What about your guests? They'll be leaving soon, I imagine."

Ginger smiled at her husband. What he meant to say was he *hoped* their departure would be soon. "I won't be long, love. I'll return after this round of drinks to say goodnight."

Unfortunately, Ginger took much longer to settle Rosa than she'd thought, and by the time she returned to the garden, the last round of drinks had been consumed and everyone had gone. Basil greeted her in the parlour. "Ah, there you are!"

"I'm so sorry, love," Ginger said. "What a terrible hostess I turned out to be. I hope no one was very upset."

"Not from what I could tell. The taxicabs arrived in a row, and the ladies left to use the bathroom, so the gentlemen had a bit of difficulty rounding them up, but everyone was successfully shuttled away. There were plenty of slurring instructions for me to wish you well and thank you for a marvellous party." Holding a hand over his mouth to stifle a yawn, he motioned to the stairs. "Shall we?"

Ginger took his arm, and they headed up the staircase, her mind reviewing the evening's highlights and somehow landing on her dance with Louis. And Basil's with Sabine Chapdelaine.

"Did you enjoy your dance with Madame Chapdelaine?" she asked with a grin.

They'd reached the landing, and Basil grabbed her by the waist. "It was deplorable." His lips found the nape of her neck. "The worst dance I've ever had in my life."

Ginger giggled at her husband's attempt to deflect what had really happened—a pleasant experience dancing with a beautiful, sophisticated lady.

He held her gaze as he pushed red locks behind her ear. "I believe she's jealous of you, Ginger."

"Whatever for?"

"I'm not sure. She seemed to believe you and that Roger fellow had a past. Of course, I told her that was impossible."

"Of course," Ginger returned. "I've never met a Roger Bernard before tonight." Then she kissed her husband, leading him to their bed. It was her turn to distract him from the truth.

3

Much like Ginger's London home Hartigan House, the high ceilings of the entrance hall created an echo chamber, and when a large party was preparing to leave, the noise was nearly deafening.

Ginger straightened Scout's cap. "You'll take good care of Boss, won't you?"

"The best, Mum," Scout said.

Boss, who seemed to have a perpetual smile on his canine face, sat on his haunches, his tongue hanging. His dark, round eyes flashed with eagerness, knowing that the leash attached to his collar and held by his young master meant an exciting adventure. Ginger swooped him up under her arm for one last fur hug before returning him to Scout.

"It feels odd to be leaving you behind," Felicia said. She looked regal in her umber-coloured Jeanne Lavine fall coat with embroidered tan stitching and matching cloche as she linked her arm with Charles'. "But I completely understand wanting to stay for the fashion parade. If Charles didn't need to get back to work, I'd beg him to let us stay."

Felicia had other reasons to return, one of which was to see her physician. Ginger worried about Felicia's constant back pain, and now she was favouring her lower stomach.

"I promise to return with a full report," Ginger said, forcing joviality. "I'll be so precise in my descriptions; you'll feel like you were there yourself."

Felicia laughed. "Ginger, you're a dear."

"And you must do exactly what the doctor says," Ginger returned. "And do rest as much as possible on your journey."

"I will," Felicia said, squeezing Ginger's arm.

Ambrosia sat on an ornate bench, her back straight due to the corset she refused to relinquish, a map of wrinkles on the soft skin of her face, and grey hair pulled back in a low bun. She leaned against a pearl-handled walking stick, gripping it with crooked fingers weighed down with rings adorned with large gems. "Remind me never to leave England again," she said, as maids and footmen bustled about as they hauled down the luggage. "Murderer on the loose in London, or not."

"Oh, Grandmother," Ginger said. "Change is as good as a rest, and I know you had a nice time here."

Ambrosia pursed her lips but didn't deny it.

"Where is Rosa?" Basil asked. He checked his pocket watch and frowned. "The taxicabs will be arriving shortly, and I'd like to say goodbye to my daughter before I leave."

Basil had reluctantly agreed to Ginger's request that she delay her departure, but he was less enthusiastic about leaving Rosa behind. Ginger loved the attachment he had to his little daughter, and even though she was certain Rosa would be fine in Nanny Green's care, she couldn't bear the thought of separating again. She had had to let her family go to France without her, Rosa included, and even though they were going back to England without her now, she didn't want to repeat the experience with her baby.

Ginger searched the hall and spotted the French maid called Cosette. Slender and in her mid-twenties, she had serious dark eyes and a mouth that pursed. "Cosette, please find Nanny Green and have her bring the baby to me." The maid bobbed in a stiff, graceless manner and scurried up the stairs.

Charles faced Basil as he slipped into his trench coat. "I imagine the Yard is eager for you to return, old chap."

"There are plenty of good men on the force," Basil said with deference. "I'm sure I wasn't missed."

Ginger chuckled. "I'm sure you were. And more to the point, you've missed working at the Yard."

Placing his trilby on his head, Basil grinned crookedly as he replied, "You know me too well, love. Indeed, Paris has a certain *je ne sais quoi*, but as they say, there's no place like home." He brushed her cheek with his and whispered, "If only you were coming with me."

"I'll be right behind you, love," Ginger whispered back. "Time will fly, and you'll hardly notice I'm gone."

Nanny Green, a sturdy woman with a competent air, arrived with Rosa on her hip and handed the child to Ginger. The red-cheeked baby gnawed on her chubby little fist as if that would soothe swollen gums.

"You poor dear," Ginger said. "We all get our teeth the same way, through suffering and struggle. Even Princess Elizabeth can't escape it."

"Oh, that's true," Felicia broke in. "I read about the baby princess' teething distress in the social pages."

Ginger kissed Rosa's head and then handed her to Basil. "Say farewell to Papa."

The taxicabs arrived—taking five to haul everyone and the luggage to the train station—and Ginger said farewells to her family as the swell moved outdoors.

Standing with Lizzie on one side and Nanny Green holding Rosa on the other, Ginger watched as Charles helped Felicia and Ambrosia into one taxicab, and as Basil and Scout with Boss got into another. The maids, Langley and Daphne, and Charles' butler, Burton, climbed into a third.

She waved as they drove away, horns honking in response, until the motorcars disappeared at the end of the drive.

The hall felt unnervingly quiet when Ginger stepped back in, and for the briefest moment, she regretted not leaving with her family.

"I'll take Rosa back to the nursery, madam," Nanny Green said. "I think all the commotion has tired her out."

Ginger nodded. "I'll be up shortly."

"Is there anything you need from me, madam?" Lizzie asked.

"I think I'd like a little time to myself," Ginger replied. "Do see if Madame Dupris needs any help in the kitchen."

"Yes, madam." Lizzie bobbed before leaving.

The villa staff waited in the wings. Ginger always took the time to learn the names of those who assisted her, and her skills in the French language made it easy to communicate. Along with Cosette were the maid Elise and the footman Beaufort.

Beaufort spoke for the three of them, asking in French, "Is there anything you'll need from us, Madame?"

"*Non, merci.*"

Ginger did want time alone, something she hadn't enjoyed since arriving in France. Though she'd invited Haley to stay the night of the party, Haley had insisted on returning to her flat precisely because she hoped to miss the hullabaloo that accompanied the waving off of such a large group. She'd politely said her goodbyes to everyone going back to London the evening before—after the other guests had left. Haley had promised to return to the villa after her work at the hospital mortuary to share dinner with Ginger. Until then,

Ginger's time was her own. She could read a book, take a nap, or even go for a swim. She'd been humble when she'd told Haley she'd only mastered the dog paddle. Frequent visits to the municipal pool in Boston had allowed Ginger to become rather proficient.

She was halfway up the white marble steps when the vestibule filled with a shrieking scream. Scurrying back down the steps, Ginger's heart raced as she searched for the source. Lizzie, wide-eyed and frantic, lifted her skirt as she ran towards Ginger.

"Oh, madam, madam!"

"Lizzie, what is it?"

As Lizzie struggled for a breath, Ginger worried the poor girl was about to faint.

"Do calm down, Lizzie," Ginger said carefully. "Take a breath and then tell me what's wrong."

Lizzie pinched her eyes as she exhaled, then looked at Ginger. "There's a body in the pool."

4

Ginger's mind immediately raced through the members of her own family, mentally counting all who had recently departed—Of those who were meant to leave, none remained, did they? No. Rosa was safe in the nursery with Nanny Green upstairs. Wasn't she? Ginger hadn't actually witnessed the nanny climb the staircase, but surely . . .

Barely registering the clicking of her heels on the marble floors, Ginger pushed through the door that led to the closed-in pool. The morning sunlight that streamed through the wall of windows reflected off the water's surface and was momentarily blinding. Ginger cupped her eyes, searched for the body, and found it floating face down. She gasped as she regis-tered the waves of short red hair.

Sabine Chapdelaine.

Oh mercy.

Ginger turned to Lizzie, who hovered by the door, and was pleased to see one of the French staff had come to see what the commotion was about.

"Elise." Ginger's voice reverberated along the high ceilings.

The maid curtsied, then noticing the body in the pool for the first time, slapped a palm over her mouth.

Ginger stepped in front of the maid, forcing her to hold her gaze. In French, she said, "Elise, please ring for the *Sûreté*. Tell them there's been a death and to come immediately."

Elise bobbed at the knees quickly before scut-tling away.

If only Haley had accepted her invitation to stay the night. At least she was only a telephone call away. The villa was equipped with a telephone, as were the police station and the hospital. Her instinct was to ring Haley immediately, but she didn't want to leave the body and chance any conta-mination of evidence, and she didn't want to ask Lizzie to stay in the pool room with a dead body.

That was certainly more than her job as a lady's maid warranted.

"Lizzie, do you think you could manage to make a telephone call to the hospital? Ask Cosette for assistance. She speaks English. Leave a message for Miss Higgins to come to the villa immediately. Say that it's urgent."

"Yes, madam," Lizzie said with a bob before disappearing.

Once the police arrived, she'd be pushed out of the way, so Ginger took this time alone in the pool room with Sabine Chapdelaine to take in the scene.

The room itself seemed in order. A few lounge chairs and a metal bistro table with two chairs were situated exactly as they should be, so there was no sign of a struggle. Stepping close to the pool's edge, Ginger tugged on her frock hem to squat and get a better look. It was difficult to see much as the lower half of the body was submerged. Both T-strap shoes remained, though Mme Chapdelaine's jewelled hair comb was lying on the bottom of the pool.

The back of her head was easiest to view, although no damage to the skull was evident.

Standing, Ginger strolled around the pool's perimeter, her mind working. Why had the designer come to the pool room? And when? She'd arrived at the party with Roger Bernard. Did they not leave together? A collection of taxicabs had been waiting, but Ginger had been called upstairs with Rosa before the last of them had left.

Ginger supposed the fashion designer might have left and returned, but that scenario seemed very unlikely.

Mme Chapdelaine had found her way to the pool room without detection and met her death. Had she slipped and fallen, hitting her head on the way in? If so, the damage would be to her forehead. Or had someone pushed her in? If the lady were a non-swimmer, she would be in trouble in the deep end. Or had she gone in of her own volition? She might have lost her inhibitions due to high alcohol consumption and lost her way. Ginger would have to wait until the body could be examined.

And what about the blue glass? As Ginger had started up the staircase the evening before, she'd noted that Mme Chapdelaine had received her drink in the blue glass. Ginger squinted as she scoured the depths of the pool. She could see nothing out of the ordinary. No glass, broken or otherwise. She searched the pool's perimeter, the patio, and the areas beneath the empty tables. There was no blue glass anywhere. Had Mme Chapdelaine disposed of it before coming into the pool room, or had the perpetrator absconded with it?

Sighing, Ginger checked her watch. The police would be there shortly.

Meanwhile, her mind listed persons to interview. As Mme Chapdelaine's date, Roger Bernard, or Louis, was on the top of the list, though Ginger hated to think he could be capable. M. and Mme Rochefort could hopefully shed some light on the situation.

Maybe Mme Chapdelaine was already dead at the point she'd gone into the pool? The Rocheforts were definitely people of interest.

The villa staff would need to be questioned. The maids Elise and Cosette, the footman Beaufort, and the cook who also operated as head housekeeper, Mme Dupris. The groundskeeper, who also looked after the pool, came a couple of times a week and hadn't been present at the time of Mme Chapdelaine's death. Someone might've seen or overheard something of note. Lizzie would be counted in that number, but she didn't understand a word of French, so Ginger didn't know if she would be much help. However, the police would thoroughly question her since she had found the body.

"Mrs. Reed?"

Ginger turned to Lizzie's breathy voice.

"Yes?"

"The police are here."

"Very good," Ginger said. "Show them in."

Before Lizzie could respond, a tall, round-chested man stepped around her, his hat in hand, a uniformed officer hovering behind him.

"You must be Madame Reed," he said in heavily accented English. He had a thick moustache and squinty brown eyes and held a bowler hat in his hands. With a slight bow, he added, "I am Inspector Tremblay. I understand misfortune has befallen you."

BEING MARRIED to a chief inspector of the Metropolitan Police, Ginger had had her fair share of acquaintances in law enforcement and had developed a quick read of character. In a matter of seconds after meeting Inspector Tremblay, in the way he dismissively pushed her aside, viewing her with suspicion, she knew they would be cautious adversaries.

"Do you know the name of this woman?" he asked.

"It's Sabine Chapdelaine."

His head snapped up. "The fashion designer?"

"Yes. Do you follow fashion, Inspector Tremblay?"

"When one lives in Paris, one can hardly miss the big names of fashion, madame."

Ginger conceded that was probably true.

The inspector had come with a uniformed officer who took notes. Inspector Tremblay cast the officer a glance as if to reassure himself that the man was doing his job, then turned back to Ginger. "Madame Chapdelaine was a guest in your home, Madame Reed?"

"She attended a party I threw last night."

"Was she imbibing alcoholic beverages?"

Ginger nodded. "She quite enjoyed the cocktails on offer. I was under the impression she had left along with the other guests."

"I must see a list of all the people who were at the party."

"Of course, but most of them were members of my family with no connection with Madame Chapdelaine. They left for England this morning."

Inspector Tremblay shot her another look. "And you did not return with them?"

"I decided to stay an extra week to attend the fashion parade."

"Hmm. I see. I believe the show will be somewhat altered now. Who discovered the body, and at what time?"

"My maid, Lizzie, found her at approximately 0700."

Inspector Tremblay removed a pipe from his pocket and rested it in the side of his mouth, unlit. "Why was your maid to be found in the pool room?"

"I'm assuming she was assisting the villa staff in tidying up after last night's party. Probably just a routine look about."

"It appears she fell in and drowned," the inspector said. "Such a shame. Madame Chapdelaine was a beauty." His eyes settled on Ginger. "Much like yourself, madame. In fact, I see a resemblance."

"Not all redheads look alike, Inspector," Ginger returned coolly, "but I will take your comparison as a compliment."

"That was, indeed, my intention, madame."

"Let's keep this professional, shall we?" Ginger said. "Is a doctor on the way?"

"You English," the inspector said with a huff of disappointment. "Stuffed shirts? Is that the correct term?"

Ginger ignored the insinuation. "I have a friend

working at the hospital mortuary. Perhaps she can help examine the body?"

Inspector Tremblay flicked his hand. "It matters not to me who confirms that this poor woman drowned in your pool." He removed his pipe and waved it about like a flag. "I will ensure the body is taken away as soon as possible so you can get on with your day and enjoy the rest of your time in Paris."

"That's it?" Ginger said, unable to keep the dismay from her voice. "That's the extent of your investigation?"

The man shrugged, then produced a box of matches. "There's no sign of a struggle, no blood. You say she was drinking at your party. Obviously, she wandered off and fell into your pool. The real crime is that no one noticed that she had gone missing."

Ginger wondered about that unfortunate fact as well.

"*Au revoir*," the inspector said on his way out. "I will wait until I am outside to light my pipe."

"Much appreciated." Ginger scowled as she stared at the back of the man's head as he left the pool room. The inspector could very well be correct about drowning as the cause of death, and most likely was. But until an autopsy proved it, he couldn't know that for certain.

Ginger hadn't much time to stew as the doctor arrived just as the inspector left.

"Madame," the doctor said as he reached out a hand. He was bald and hunched over with small brown eyes that lit up, even at the sight of a body. Ginger supposed it was good that the man enjoyed his job serving the dead. He continued with a slight lisp. "I overheard you speak English. Is that what you prefer?"

"If you are comfortable with it," Ginger said.

"I am Dr. Lyon." He pronounced it *LEEon*.

"I am Madame Reed."

Dr. Lyon stared at the body still floating in the pool. "And this poor woman did not have a good night."

"Indeed, she did not."

The doctor had brought along two youthful and strong-looking assistants. In French, he instructed them to remove the body from the pool. Ginger watched as they fished Mme Chapdelaine out of the pool, her face bloated and white, her lips blue, and her eyes open. The tepid water darkened the floor as it spread out from the body in slick, wet puddles.

5

Ginger caught Haley's attention as she walked in.

"Thank goodness. You're here."

"A death?" Haley said. She wore masculine trousers unapologetically. "Lizzie did sound frantic, so I suppose I shouldn't be surprised." Stepping closer to peer around the doctor and the attendants, she added, "Ah . . . the lovely Madame Chapdelaine." Haley settled dark eyes on Ginger. "Any idea how she ended up here?"

Ginger shook her head. "None at all."

Haley's gaze landed on the attending physician. "It's Dr. Lyon," she said. "I'm one of his students."

"That's fantastic." Ginger nudged her with her elbow. "Go and offer your services."

"I'd be happy to."

Haley approached the doctor and extended her hand. Speaking slowly in French, she said, "I'm Miss Higgins. I'm a student from America doing my practicum at the Hôtel-Dieu."

Recognition flickered behind his eyes. "Yes," the doctor returned in English. "I've seen you at my lectures. The only female, if I am correct."

"Sadly, that is true."

Dr. Lyon grinned. "Rather tall for a lady, eh?"

"The topic has come up once or twice," Haley said. "I'm a friend of Mrs. Reed. She'd be pleased if I could be of assistance, and I would love the opportunity to study this case with you."

"Inspector Tremblay believes it to be an accident," Dr. Lyon said.

"Do you?" Haley asked.

Dr. Lyon lifted a shoulder. "Do *you*?"

Haley moved to the body, tugged her trousers, and squatted for a closer look. Ginger stepped in behind, observing with curiosity.

Haley placed two palms on the corpse's chest and pushed. Glancing at the doctor, she said, "There doesn't appear to be any water in the lungs."

Dr. Lyon looked pleased. "The body was floating

near the surface, suggesting that the lungs were acting like buoys."

"She didn't drown?" Ginger asked.

"It's not definitive, as a person can drown in a surprisingly small amount of water." Haley carefully pushed the blue lips of the corpse open and stared into the mouth. "The cavity membranes of her mouth are inflamed."

Ginger raised a brow. "She'd ingested poison?"

"It's a possibility." Haley stood, smoothing out her trousers. She turned to Dr. Lyon. "Since the cause of death is in question, I'm assuming a post-mortem is reasonable?"

"I concur, Miss Higgins," Dr. Lyon said with a nod of his bald head. "It's the only way to be certain that a crime hasn't occurred here."

"What about Inspector Tremblay?" Ginger asked. "He pretty much wiped his hands clean of the situation."

Dr. Lyon rolled his small eyes as if he were used to dealing with Inspector Tremblay's arrogance. "I'll release my findings to the commissaire. Madame Chapdelaine was a prominent Parisian citizen. He'll want the truth."

With the doctor's go-ahead, the two attendants lifted the covered body of Mme Chapdelaine onto a stretcher and wheeled her out of the pool room. Ginger presumed an ambulance was waiting outside.

Dr. Lyon approached Ginger with a smile. "It was a pleasure to meet you, madame. So sorry it was under these unfortunate circumstances."

"The pleasure is mine," Ginger returned. "I have a feeling we'll see each other again soon."

"I hope so," Dr. Lyon said. With slumped shoulders, he turned to leave the pool room, pausing to address Haley. "Miss Higgins, are you coming?"

"Absolutely." Haley shot Ginger a look and stepped quickly after the doctor.

"Don't forget I have a telephone here," Ginger said, calling after her friend.

Haley waved. "I know."

6

Ginger wished she could've tagged along with Haley to the mortuary, but her friend was competent and would report back to her anything of import. That didn't mean Ginger would default to her original plan of reading a book and taking a nap, and she definitely wouldn't be going for a swim.

No. She would take the time to speak to the villa staff. A guest of hers had died under her watch—Ginger's instinct made her believe the event was nefarious—and she'd do what she could to track down the killer in the week she remained in Paris.

The villa kitchen was impressively large, though not as large as the one at Hartigan House. A large white porcelain sink was built into wooden cupboards, a large table in the centre had a rack for hanging copper-bottomed pans above it, open shelves displayed the villa dishware, and a small refrigerator stood near the back entrance.

Ginger found Mme Dupris flipping through a recipe book with the intensity of a person whose passions were inflamed by the content matter she read. The head cook's skills were next to none, and dining at the villa had been a pleasure shared by Ginger's whole family, even the curmudgeonly Ambrosia, who'd made it clear she preferred a simple English meal to the butter-heavy concoctions of the French.

Mme Dupris either had a speedy metabolism or discipline that kept her from consuming her works of art, as she possessed a slender frame one wouldn't naturally attribute to someone in her line of work. She wore a pale blue day frock under a white apron and had a white cook's hat on her head. When she spotted Ginger, she got to her feet then said in French, "Ah, Madame Reed, is it true? Did she pass away?"

Mme Dupris didn't bother stating *who* had died, so clearly, the news had spread amongst the staff.

"*Oui*," Ginger continued in French. "I'm afraid Madame Chapdelaine has died." Ginger waved to the chair. "Please do sit. You don't mind if I join you?"

Mme Dupris blinked in surprise. It wasn't customary for the kitchen staff to mingle with the guests.

"I only want to ask a few questions," Ginger clarified as she took an empty chair. "Madame Chapdelaine was my guest, and I hope I can find out what happened to her."

Mme Dupris nodded, then reclaimed her chair. "It is a terrible accident, no?"

Ginger avoided answering and said, "I'm wondering if you or the others happened to see anything out of the ordinary."

Huffing, Mme Dupris said, "I see nothing. I was in the kitchen the whole time."

"What about the maids or the footman," Ginger said. "Did any of them mention anything?"

"It is our job to be discreet, madame"

At the cook's sour look, Ginger thought it might help to add a little praise. "Like you, they do such an excellent job. You've trained them well. It's as if they're invisible to the guests. Perhaps they overheard something that was said. I wouldn't ask if this tragedy hadn't occurred. In this instance, no one would accuse you of having a loose tongue."

At the mention of the word, the cook clicked her tongue. "You will have to ask them yourself, madame. Like I said, I was busy working for your party."

If Mme Dupris knew anything, she wasn't about to tell Ginger. No doubt she'd open up to the police.

Ginger changed tactics.

"Who was responsible for preparing the cocktails?"

"Elise and Cosette. Perhaps Beaufort assisted."

"Is it usual for the maids and footman to mix drinks? I assumed a barman would be hired for the occasion."

"We had one lined up, madame. Monsieur Denis Faucher, who also works at La Petite Porte Rouge, cancelled at the last minute. Claims he had a stomach ailment."

"You don't believe him?"

"Certainly, I do. He has many children and would not miss the chance to make money unless it was an emergency."

This fact would account for Ginger's guests giving less than stellar reviews of the drinks, though the longer the night went on, the less they complained.

"Does the villa hold a set of cocktail glasses that have a blue tint?" Ginger asked.

Mme Dupris wrinkled a brow. "No. There is no such thing in this kitchen."

"Are you certain?"

Mme Dupris' eyes darkened, clearly slighted. "I know every single article in this house. We have clear glassware only."

Ginger glanced around the kitchen, registering that she and the cook remained alone. "Where would I find Elise or Cosette?"

"They are cleaning up after the guests who have departed." Mme Dupris stared blankly at Ginger. "I presume you'll still want dinner prepared tonight, Madame Reed."

Ginger pushed away from the table, and the cook did the same. "Yes, please. Miss Higgins will be joining us."

"Very well, madame. I'll put out a tray of sandwiches for lunch."

Ginger checked her watch. No wonder her stomach was gurgling; it was nearly noon.

"Thank you, Madame Dupris," she said. "It'll just be me for lunch. Nanny Green and baby Rosa will need to be attended to as usual."

With her hands clasped in front of her apron, Mme Dupris nodded. "Of course, madame."

When Ginger found Cosette Padou, she was finishing the bedroom Ambrosia had stayed in. She stared at Ginger with a peculiar look, an odd mix of deference and defiance with narrow eyes and tight lips. Perhaps she held an underlying prejudice against the British. Many French did, despite an alliance between the two countries during the Great War. Or perhaps it was just an illusion brought on by the slight lack of symmetry in her face. One cheekbone seemed more pronounced than the other—perhaps related to the presence of a thin silvery scar?

"Hello, Cosette," Ginger said with a smile.

Cosette had made it known to Ginger that she could speak English "a leetle beet" on their first meeting.

"Madame Reed," Cosette said with a curtsey. "You look well."

Ginger thought it an odd salutation coming from a maid but wrote it off as nerves. "Thank you. As you've most likely heard, we had a guest perish in the villa last night."

The maid replied with a thick accent. "Yes, madame, I did hear. So terrible."

"I'm trying to put together the last moments of Madame Chapdelaine's life, and I'm hoping you can help."

"*Me*, madame? I do not know how."

"You, Elise, and Beaufort did a wonderful job waiting on the guests during the garden party."

"Thank you, madame."

"You were so smooth and quiet that people like my guests, especially when they've been in their cups . . ."

"In their cups, madame?"

"When they've been drinking alcohol."

"Yes, of course. I am sorry to interrupt."

Ginger switched to French. "Not at all. You must understand me clearly, so please speak up if you don't."

"I will," Cosette returned in English.

"Like I said, people in that situation often forget that the maids and footmen are in their midst and don't always guard their speech."

"You want to know if I heard something spoken against Mme Chapdelaine?"

Ginger inclined her head. "Did you?"

Cosette's lips tightened against her teeth, her eyes flashing as though she was in deep deliberation.

"I appreciate your commitment to discretion," Ginger said. "But a person has died. In this situation, your honesty will be forgiven."

Cosette worked her lips and said, "I overheard Madame Rochefort and Madame Miller talking about Madame Chapdelaine."

"What did they say?" Ginger asked.

"They were unhappy with how their husbands were circling Madame Chapdelaine, '*comme les loups*', Madame Miller said. Like wolves. Madame Rochefort scoffed and said, "*She* is the wolf.""

"I see," Ginger said. Jealously was a common motive for many domestic murders. "I understand that you, Elise, and Beaufort were tasked with making the cocktails."

"*Oui, madame*. M. Faucher cancelled at the last moment. There was no time to find someone else." She stared at Ginger over dark lashes. "I hope the drinks were to your satisfaction."

"They were satisfactory," Ginger said. "What do you know about a blue glass?"

Cosette frowned. "I do not understand."

"There was a blue glass in circulation last night,"

Ginger returned. "Madame Dupris claims to know nothing about it."

"Nor do I, madame." Cosette seemed as if she wanted to speak but was afraid to.

"Is there something you want to tell me, Cosette?" Ginger said. "Please feel free."

"Very well, madame. Are you certain the glass was blue? Perhaps a play with the lighting made it appear so?"

Ginger had begun to wonder that herself. Perhaps there never was a blue glass, and she had imagined a clue where there wasn't one.

"Do you recall who delivered Madame Chapdelaine's final drink?"

Cosette's eyes rounded at the question. "Was madame poisoned?"

"Why do you ask that, Cosette?"

"Oh, well, only because of your question about the drink. Forgive me for jumping to conclusions."

"As it is, the cause of death is yet to be determined. I'm only curious, Cosette. Do you recall?"

"I believe it was Elise, but we were all making and delivering drinks. Your guests were rather demanding towards the end of the evening."

Ginger stared in surprise at the maid's forwardness.

Cosette's gaze dropped to the floor. "Forgive me, madame, but you did ask for honesty."

"Indeed, I did. And I thank you." Ginger gave a slight nod. "If you think of anything else that might help, please do seek me out."

Cosette bobbed at the knees. "Yes, madame."

"Now, where might I find Elise?"

The corner of Cosette's mouth turned up. "Elise is cleaning the lavatory. She lost the coin toss."

Ginger went in search of Elise; however, the maid wasn't in the lavatory when Ginger got there. She did find Lizzie tidying up the room she had shared with Basil, energetically fluffing the duvet and straightening it with sharp slaps.

"Lizzie?" Ginger said. "Are you all right?"

Lizzie's small, mouse-like features were strained, her skin even more pale than usual. She pivoted towards Ginger and bowed. "Madam." Her bottom lip trembled.

"Lizzie," Ginger said with a sense of alarm. "You've suffered a shock. Why don't you take the afternoon off."

"That's kind of you, madam, but keeping busy helps keep my mind off home."

Keeping her eyes on her maid, Ginger ducked her chin. "Are you homesick?"

"I think so, madam. I've never been away from my mum or brothers and sisters for so long. And with Madame Chapdelaine . . ."

"Lizzie, I want to have lunch in the nursery today with Nanny Green and Rosa. Would you mind collecting it from Madame Dupris?"

"Of course, madam."

"Splendid. And I need you there as well, so please be sure there's enough food for you as well."

Lizzie blinked. "You want *me* to eat in the nursery with you?"

"Why not? Saves you traipsing up and down the stairs if I should need you for something."

Lizzie almost smiled. "Very well, madam, if that's what you wish."

7

Haley rode with Dr. Lyon in his boxy '22 Renault that had sharper lines than its British or American counterpart. As they followed the ambulance from the villa to the hospital mortuary, she bit the inside of her lip the entire time to keep from breaking into an inappropriate smile. It was unbecoming to feel joy at the expense of another person's death.

Still, here she was, about to perform an autopsy with Dr. Lyon, an expert in the science of pathology. Haley had been keen to return to Europe to study because most advancements in toxicology were coming from there, and Dr. Lyon was highly esteemed by his colleagues in chemical analysis.

It was unfortunate this corpse had been a guest of Ginger's, but it also put Haley in the unique situation of having known the victim, if briefly. Certainly long enough to witness the abuse Mme Chapdelaine was doing to her liver through copious alcohol consumption.

"Thank you for allowing me to tag along, Dr. Lyon," Haley said. "I realise this is an unconventional situation."

"I will tell you the truth, Miss Higgins. I would not have requested your assistance had you not been at the top of your class. I can hardly ignore your intelligence."

It took a lot for Haley to experience an emotional reaction to words, but she found Dr. Lyon's praise caused her cheeks to heat up. To battle against it, she focused on the view of Paris out the window. There was no missing the Eiffel Tower, which at night was lit with a large Citroën sign running vertically. Easily the tallest structure in the city, the iconic tower could be seen from everywhere.

The doctor followed her gaze. "Ah, a masterpiece, is it not?"

Haley had to nod in acknowledgement. "It is."

"It's the tallest building in the whole world!"

The man's pride was enthusiastic and childlike, and Haley couldn't help but grin.

When they finally pulled up to the hospital, Haley followed Dr. Lyon, easily seeing over the short man's head as they headed to the basement where the mortuary was situated.

Haley had been inside many mortuaries, or morgues as they were referred to back home in Boston, and they all found their homes in the basements of hospitals. New electric lamps replaced the gaslight versions that helped to light the dim room, which might have small but high windows at street level. All smelled of death and musty dampness, an occupational hazard with which Haley had long ago made peace.

The ambulance attendants wheeled the gurney into the mortuary and then lifted Mme Chapdelaine's body onto the ceramic table. Dr. Lyon signed the papers, which would be delivered to the hospital administration, then sent the attendants on their way.

Finally, Haley, Dr. Lyon, and the corpse were alone.

Haley couldn't have been more thrilled.

"Let's prepare," Dr. Lyon said.

Haley pulled two clean aprons out of a set of cabinet drawers and handed one to Dr. Lyon. After tying it securely at her back, she removed the rubber band from her hair, wincing as it ripped out a few strands and the hairpins that held up a faux bob. Drawing her nuisance curls off her face, she used the rubber band to create a ponytail and the pins to keep any strays off her face. Next, she headed to the sink, thoroughly scrubbing her hands with carbolic soap and water.

The bald Dr. Lyon did not need to fuss with a halo of curls and was ready and waiting. He nodded towards the body, and Haley understood he wanted her to start. She removed the sheet, pausing for a moment as she took in Mme Chapdelaine's lifeless form.

"A shame," Dr. Lyon said. "Such a vibrant beauty, gone too soon."

When it came to making the Y-incision, Haley never squirmed. Still, the initial removal of a victim's clothing always gave her a sense of unease, as if she was about to violate a person most intimately.

"Look at her shoulders," Dr. Lyon said, understanding. "Not the face, and not, er, below."

Haley followed the instructions and found that it

worked. Once she'd cut the clothing off the body, it became just that. The body. Mme Chapdelaine disappeared along with her damp clothing and jewellery, which were deposited in a bag that would end up with the police.

Dr. Lyon then pointed at a sterilised scalpel on a nearby tray.

"Would you like to do the honours, Miss Higgins?"

"I would, thank you."

Replacing the sheet to cover the lower half of the body, Haley took the scalpel and carefully carved out the large Y. She and Dr. Lyon would remove all the essential organs, the ones below the ribcage, then with the help of a small saw, the lungs and the heart to follow.

"The blood appears rather dark," Haley said.

"Hmm, yes," Dr. Lyon said.

Haley added, "The stomach and intestines are reddened and inflamed."

"*Oui*, I see."

"All the organs have obvious clumps of bulbous blood in the vessels," Haley said with interest. "Particularly the liver."

"*Oui*, it was damaged by the alcohol beforehand," Dr. Lyon said.

"We can't rule out poison, but there aren't many poisons that would work this quickly and produce this kind of evidence."

Dr. Lyon squinted at Haley. "Do you have a theory, Miss Higgins?"

"I do," Haley said, "but I'd like to run a test first."

"I will begin with the brain," Dr. Lyon said. "I presume you would like the liver?"

"I would." Haley carefully handled the liver and sliced a section. What she did next wasn't that much different from what a chef might do when making pâté or sauce. She minced the tissue, then distilled it with steam. The resulting syrup-like substance, with the addition of lye and benzene, was brought to a boil and watched as it turned yellowish red.

"How is it?" Dr. Lyon asked.

"I'm ready to subject it to fluorescent light." Haley put the sample under the light, and the soupy sauce turned a yellowish green. She flashed the pathologist a broad smile of success. "It's positive for poison, Dr. Lyon."

AFTER A PLEASANT LUNCHEON in the nursery, Ginger continued her search for Elise and found her in the laundry room, ironing sheets.

"*Bonjour*, Elise," Ginger said lightly to avoid startling the maid.

Elise's blonde hair was tucked under a maid's cap, baring her long neck. Her hazel-eyed gaze shot up, widening as she registered Ginger in an area where guests rarely entered. She bobbed quickly, then said in French, "Are you lost, madame?"

"No," Ginger said with a quick shake of her head. She returned in French, "I was looking for you."

"Oh?" Elise stared, wide-eyed. "How might I be of assistance?"

"I would like to ask you a couple of questions regarding last night."

Elise's gaze moved to her hands, cupped tightly at her waist. "Poor Madame Chapdelaine. Such a tragedy."

"Indeed. With the barman absent, you, Cosette, and Beaufort were kept rather busy."

"Yes, madame. The cocktails were in high demand."

Ginger knew this to be true—her French guests, Mme Chapdelaine in particular, liked their drinks. And her American guests, Haley excluded, seemed to be making up for time lost to Prohibition.

"Do you recall taking a drink to Madame Chapdelaine?"

"I took several drinks to her and her companion, Monsieur Bernard." The maid's expression soured as she mentioned Louis.

"Is there something about Monsieur Bernard that troubles you?"

"Oh, I would never presume to mention, madame"

"I understand. I only want to discover the truth about what happened last night. You won't get into trouble. I promise."

"It was nothing, I am sure," Elise said. "He didn't like how the other men fawned over Madame Chapdelaine—it's understandable—she was such a beautiful lady."

"What made you think Monsieur Bernard was bothered by that?" Ginger asked.

"There was a change in the song, and he took her arm and forced her to dance."

"And you don't believe Madame Chapdelaine was agreeable?"

"Not at first. Monsieur Bernard had tugged her arm roughly, and she scowled back at him. But then, once they were dancing, it appeared all was forgiven."

"At what point did you bring Madame Chapdelaine her last drink?" Ginger asked. "Was it after that dance with Monsieur Bernard?"

"Who said I was the one to give her the final drink?" Elise said with a frown.

"Cosette suggested it," Ginger replied.

Elise scoffed as she rolled her eyes. "Cosette."

"Do you have a low regard for Cosette?"

"Cosette thinks she's better than everyone else, cleverer than us all, and yet she is a maid, the same as me."

There was no love lost between maids, Ginger mused. She inclined her head. "Was she wrong? Did you not give Madame Chapdelaine her last drink?"

After a sigh, Elise nodded. "I believe I did." Her chin shot up. "But you don't think I—?"

"I'm only trying to put the order of events together, Elise." Ginger smiled, attempting to put the young maid at ease. "Did you make the drink yourself?"

"Not that time."

"Who made it?"

Elise's forehead crumpled. "Honestly, madame, I don't remember. It was such a busy evening."

Elise stood stiffly, her eyes appealing to Ginger to

allow her to return to her work, which looked like a lot.

"Thank you, Elise," Ginger said. "You've been very helpful."

Elise curtsied, then returned to her tasks.

8

*T*he footman, Beaufort, was in the boot room polishing the shoes, the polish leaving the space with a pleasant scent. Beaufort, his height causing him to look awkward as he bent forward, jumped to attention when he saw Ginger. Bowing, he said, "Madame Reed."

"*Bonjour*, Beaufort," Ginger said. "Could I have a moment of your time?" she asked in French.

"Most certainly, madame."

"It's about last night."

Beaufort offered words of condolence. "Such a beautiful lady. A tremendous loss."

Ginger understood Mme Chapdelaine had been a great beauty, but there was more to a person than appearances. With a slight nod, she said, "All loss of life is to be mourned."

"*Oui, madame.*"

"Can you tell me what transpired last night, Beaufort, from your perspective?"

Beaufort offered a soft shrug. "It was a garden party. The girls and I served then cleaned away used dishes. It was a normal affair."

"Did you hear anything that might shed light on what transpired?"

"I'm afraid I don't understand. Madame Chapdelaine liked her cocktails and perhaps had one too many. In her state, she wandered into the pool room and fell in." Beaufort let his gaze rest on Ginger. "Is this not so?"

"Madame Chapdelaine's death is under investigation. Do you remember if you made her final cocktail, or was it one of the maids?

Beaufort inhaled as his gaze turned upwards. "I'm afraid I don't recall. Very many cocktails were made last night."

"I noticed the use of a glass with a blue tint," Ginger said. "Do you know where it came from?"

Beaufort worked his lips as he slowly shook his head. "I do not recall such a glass. At least, a blue glass might not look blue once a colourful drink was inside it."

Ginger fought back a sense of frustration. Her enquiries were getting her nowhere. And if it hadn't been for Haley's suspicion of possible poisoning, Ginger would've assumed Mme Chapdelaine's death had been a drunken accident.

"How long have you worked at this villa?"

"Three years, madame."

"Were Elise and Cosette working here at the time you arrived?"

"Elise was, yes. Cosette is new. But there have been plenty of maids come through. The job at the villa depends on how often it is rented out. We all work for more than one employer."

"I see." Ginger propped a hand on her hip. "Did you happen to overhear or see anything that would cause you to feel concern for Madame Chapdelaine's welfare?"

Beaufort puckered his lips. "Well, I wouldn't like to speak out of turn, but if you insist. Perhaps I noticed this because I, too, am a man, but Monsieur Miller behaved like he believed he'd married the wrong sister."

"I beg your pardon?" Ginger said. "Whose sister?"

"Madame Chapdelaine and Madame Miller are sisters, madame. Did you not know?"

Ginger had not known. Curiously, when Sabine Chapdelaine had asked Ginger to invite the Millers, she had failed to mention the family relationship. "How do you know that, Beaufort?"

"Madame Chapdelaine is very popular in Paris, and everyone knows everything about her. You only have to pick up the latest magazine." He waved a hand in a straight line as if he envisioned a headline. "Sister of Madame Chapdelaine visits from America."

Ginger felt horrified for Aurélie Miller. Imagine coming from America to visit your sister, only to have her murdered during your stay.

Then her thoughts went to Cosette's account of Mrs. Miller's behaviour, how she and Mme Rochefort had watched Mme Chapdelaine with vitriol. Perhaps things weren't so loving between sisters.

Ginger felt she had held the footman captive for long enough, but two things happened before she could release him. The sound of motorcar engines coming up the drive prompted a look out of the window and viewing a police vehicle approaching the villa, and Elise arriving to announce that Ginger had a telephone call.

"I'll see to the front door, madame," Beaufort said.

"Please do," Ginger said, then left for the sitting room where an old-style candlestick telephone was installed. Holding the base in one hand and the cone receiver pressed to her ear with the other, she answered by announcing her name, "Madame Reed."

"Ginger, good."

Ginger smiled at the sound of Haley's voice. "Haley, hello. Have you learned the cause of death?"

"I have. Madame Chapdelaine was definitely poisoned."

"With what?"

"Chloroform."

"Interesting," Ginger replied. Chloroform was commonly used as a narcosis inducer to render patients unconscious before surgery, but its use had become increasingly controversial as deaths relating to chloroform were rather high. Ginger had a basic knowledge of chemistry and was familiar with the emergence of the periodic table of elements in the previous century. But one didn't have to understand the chemical make-up—a combination of carbon, hydrogen, and chlorine—to be aware of its dangers.

"Am I to deduce that someone enticed her to enter the pool room, held a cloth doused in chloroform to her mouth, then pushed her into the pool once unconscious?"

"Unfortunately, it's not that simple. The poison was ingested, not inhaled."

"Our original hypothesis was correct," Ginger said. "Poison in the cocktail."

"Has the glass been located?"

Ginger's attention was drawn to the noise in the entrance hall. Her "guest" had been given access.

"It has not," Ginger said, "and has quite likely been thoroughly washed at this point. I'm afraid I have to let you go. The police have returned."

"Yes. Dr. Lyon felt compelled to call them the minute we proved harmful intent. Is it our friend Tremblay?"

Ginger could see through the doorway into the sunlit hall. The silhouette of a bowler hat and the long, curved stem of a pipe and bowl tucked into the side of his mouth gave him away. "It is he."

"Would you like me to come over?" Haley asked.

"If Dr. Lyon can spare you."

"I'll flag down a taxicab," Haley returned. "I should arrive shortly. Try to stall him."

Ginger replaced the cone receiver to the candlestick stand, then smoothed out her frock, a lemon-yellow Jeanne Paquin with a gold embroidered ribbon belting the hips and featuring an oriental print on the flower-petal hemline. Pushing her shoulders back, she forced a smile, then stepped into the entrance hall.

"*Bonjour*, Inspector Tremblay," she said. "I'm guessing this isn't a social call."

"Not at all, Madame Reed. I fear I have the worst news. The exquisite Madame Chapdelaine was poisoned!"

"That is dreadful news! You must come in." She turned to Beaufort, who waited by the door. "Please have coffee delivered to the parlour."

"*Merci*," Inspector Tremblay said, slipping his pipe into the pocket of his trench coat.

Beaufort nodded and headed towards the kitchen.

The parlour walls were papered in light and dark green patterns, contrasting with a brick fireplace. The wooden furniture was upholstered with embossed rose and yellow velour.

Ginger selected a chair, crossed her legs at the

ankles, and cupped her hands on her lap. She leaned towards the inspector, hoping to put the man at ease. "So, tell me what you know, Inspector."

Inspector Tremblay grinned. "Aren't I supposed to be asking *you* that?"

Ginger chuckled. "Of course. I'm used to working with my husband. He's a chief inspector at Scotland Yard."

"*Oui*, I am aware of your husband." Inspector Tremblay scratched his chin. "Chief Inspector Basil Reed is renowned in London, as are you, Lady Gold."

Ginger was rather impressed. "You've discovered my titled name, which I received from my late husband, Daniel, Lord Gold."

"He passed away in the Great War, eh?"

"Sadly."

"You are now Madame Reed, or in England, Mrs. Reed, but you kept your title to work a little investigative business on the side?"

"You've done your homework, I see."

"*Oui, madame*. And, though the British police do not seem to mind the lady interfering in their investigations, you will understand that such liberties will not be extended to you here in France."

He grinned, but his eyes remained flat.

"I would never presume to do such a thing," Ginger said, reciprocating with a similar insincere smile.

Cosette arrived with coffee on a tray and set it on the short table between Ginger and the inspector. Ginger took her time pouring the coffee as she glanced at her wristwatch. Twenty minutes had passed since she'd come off the telephone with Haley.

"Milk, Inspector? Or sugar?"

"Both, please, madame."

With a sloth-like pace, Ginger poured milk into both cups, added a teaspoon of sugar to each, then stirred. Inspector Tremblay shifted in his seat restlessly. He sighed when Ginger finally handed him his cup.

"*Merci, madame*," the inspector said, then after a small sip, added, "*Excellent.*"

Ginger agreed. "Madame Dupris, the cook and housekeeper, is an expert at her job."

"We can agree on that," Inspector Tremblay said, then he surprised Ginger by asking, "Now tell me, how is it that the American, Miss Haley Higgins, came to be one of the guests at your garden party?"

9

The inspector's question inferring that Haley had something to do with Mme Chapdelaine's death unnerved Ginger, but she kept her cool. "We are old friends from America," she said in French, "as I spent many years living in the States, Boston to be precise." Ginger intended to stall by gracing the inspector with plenty of information he hadn't asked for. If he was intent on accusing Haley, then she had the right to be present to defend herself. "Have you been?" she asked, then continued before he could answer. "Boston has a distinctly European feel, more England than the continent to be sure, and yet rather American as well, being the new world and all. There are areas devoted to specific ethnicities: Italians, Irish, Jewish, and

Germans." She placed a finger to her chin. "Not many French that I can recall. They tend to migrate further south towards New Orleans."

"Madame Reed," Inspector Tremblay interjected with a hint of exasperation. "Perhaps you suffer from, how do you say, *la nostalgie?*

"Nostalgia?"

"*Oui,* of the home."

"Oh, you mean homesickness."

"*Oui,* homesickness. But the matter at hand—"

The sound of a motorcar coming down the drive drew Ginger and the inspector's attention to the window, and Ginger let out a breath of relief when Haley stepped out of a taxicab.

Inspector Tremblay frowned. "It appears that I can ask Miss Higgins myself."

"Surely, you must prefer that," Ginger said. She rang the bell and when Elise arrived, Ginger asked for more coffee and an extra cup.

Beaufort guided Haley to the parlour, and Ginger stood to greet her. "Why, this is a surprise! Come, you must join the inspector and me for coffee."

Inspector Tremblay stood and nodded in Haley's direction. "Miss Higgins. A pleasure to see you, and rather fortuitous, as I'm not here on a social visit."

Ginger smoothed out the back of her frock as she lowered herself into her chair. Haley took a spot on the empty sofa, tugging slightly on her trousers as she crossed her legs. She'd forgone the faux bob she often wore, with her long curls tied back into a low ponytail. Inspector Tremblay rubbed his chin, which was already shadowed with dark bristles.

Once Haley's coffee arrived and Ginger and the inspector had topped up their cups with hotter brew, Inspector Tremblay commanded the floor.

"Ladies, I am here because I have a murder to solve. Mademoiselle Higgins, I understand that you assisted Dr. Lyon with the autopsy, yes?"

Haley nodded. "I'm impressed with how quickly news travels between departments."

Inspector Tremblay grinned, his eyes flashing with pride. "Oh, yes, the *préfecture de police* is very efficient, like they now say, a well-oiled machine! With the Hôtel-Dieu hospital and Notre-Dame cathedral next door, we are a trio on the *Île de la Cité*. The *Sûreté*, the doctors, and the priests working together."

Ginger had to agree. The island in the River Seine was a spectacular canvas of impressive architecture, and the French Gothic Notre-Dame Cathedral was second to none.

Inspector Tremblay's expression darkened. "And we know our dear Madame Chapdelaine was poisoned, yes? With the chloroform."

"That's correct," Haley said. "It was ingested, not inhaled."

Ginger nodded in understanding. "Which means it must have been added to her drink some-time towards the end of the evening."

"*Oui, oui.*" Inspector Tremblay scratched his chin. "Which makes me ask who would have easy access to chloroform?" He settled his gaze on Haley. "A medical person, no?"

"Yes," Haley admitted. "Chloroform is widely used for anaesthetic purposes, though not as often as a few years ago. It's going out of favour precisely because of its highly lethal qualities."

Inspector Tremblay drew his pipe out of his pocket. "So, you admit you had access to the poison."

Haley narrowed her eyes. "Are you accusing me of something, Inspector?"

Instead of answering, the inspector lit his pipe, waiting until after his first puff to ask Ginger, "For-give me, madame, it is all right if I smoke?"

Ginger nodded with a slight shrug. The villa didn't belong to her, and she was vacating in a week anyway, so the smell of smoke in the air was only a temporary inconvenience. As the inspector continued to draw on his pipe, she took the opportunity to update Haley on what had transpired before the inspector arrived.

"Inspector Tremblay has heard of my work consulting with Scotland Yard and running my own investigative office, but he has made it clear that he's not interested in the help of a lady."

"I see," Haley said with a hint of mirth. "Troublesome interlopers, we are."

"Madame! Mademoiselle!" the inspector proclaimed with a throaty sputter. "You misunderstand me. I do request your cooperation, but you must, please, leave the investigation up to me and my men."

"Of course," Ginger said. "How is your investigation progressing, Inspector?"

"It is in the early stages, madame," he said. "Now, please, if you would answer a few questions. When did you notice that Madame Chapdelaine was missing?"

"Clearly, we didn't know she was missing," Ginger said. "My maid found her in the morning during regular cleaning duties."

The inspector tapped the bowl of his pipe with

his fingernail. "Were you not present to wish your guests *au revoir?*"

"Even though it was a small party," Ginger started, "I could not see everyone off. I have an infant daughter, and I happened to be upstairs taking care of her when the last of my guests left. I assumed Madame Chapdelaine was amongst them."

"I left early," Haley said. "I didn't see anyone leaving."

Inspect Tremblay raised a thick brow. "Oh? Why leave so soon? Were you not having a good time? I understand Americans enjoy letting go of the shackles of Prohibition." He clicked his tongue with obvious disdain.

"I came to study medicine," Haley said. "I prefer smaller, quieter groups."

"No one is quieter than the dead," the inspector quipped.

With a blank expression, Haley said, "Precisely."

"More coffee?" Ginger interjected. When the inspector shook his head, she offered a smile. "I can vouch for Miss Higgins' character, Inspector. And might I point out she lacks a motive? Why would she want Madame Chapdelaine dead? They'd never met before last night, and as you can see—" Ginger waved in Haley's direction. "Miss Higgins is hardly concerned about fashion. And you must concede that chloroform is accessible to the common man. In fact, I've heard it can be made in one's own home if one has the knowledge."

Inspector Tremblay sniffed, then lifted himself to his feet, his pipe tucked into the corner of his mouth. "I will be sending an officer over to look around. I trust you'll give him access to the villa and the grounds, Madame Reed."

Ginger stood and walked him to the entrance hall. "Whatever you need, Inspector."

Beaufort opened the main door, and Ginger crossed her arms in a huff as the inspector left. On her return to Haley, who remained languid on the parlour sofa, she said, "The nerve!"

"I don't relish the idea of spending time in a French prison," Haley said. "Do they have capital punishment in France? They do, don't they?"

Ginger sighed heavily as she fell back into her chair. "Yes, indeed. The guillotine."

10

After Inspector Tremblay had left, Haley volunteered to move into the villa.

"I thought you needed to be close to the hospital?" Ginger said with a slight arch of her red brow.

That had been an excuse, and Haley was fairly sure Ginger knew it. The villa had been overfull with Ginger's family with no hope of finding a quiet corner anywhere. "This is close enough. I don't like the thought of you staying in the big house alone with a killer on the loose."

"I'm capable of taking care of myself," Ginger said in a way that was both humble and haughty—Haley didn't know how her friend pulled that off.

"But," Ginger started, "I do have others to think about, and another competent person on the premises would be most welcome. And, of course, just having your company is a joy."

Haley spent the next couple of hours returning to her apartment to gather things she'd need for a week's stay at the villa and moving into one of the spare bedrooms down the hallway from Ginger. Dinner was served at seven o'clock, and though she and Ginger were eager to continue talking about the case, they kept the conversation light since the housemaids were up and about.

"Is the fashion parade still happening?" Haley asked. "With, you know . . ."

"It is," Ginger said. "Madame Chapdelaine was one of the main draws to the show, and her autumn line is highly anticipated. Her charisma will be missed."

Haley waved an arm dramatically. "The show must go on."

"Indeed," Ginger said. "Apparently, a memorial will be set up at the event for those who wish to honour her."

Haley pursed her lips, moving them side to side, her gaze looking blankly to the floor.

Ginger patted her friend's arm. "Is everything all right?"

"Oh, yes. I was just thinking that maybe I should go to the show."

"*That* was what was causing you such consternation?" Ginger said with a chuckle. "The fashion parade?"

"For some of us, the idea of mingling with fashion-minded people is akin to an endurance test."

"Ha. You'd rather spend the evening reading a medical tome."

"Precisely." Haley pushed dark curls behind her ears. "It's a lot to give up in exchange for hours of banter over exotic fabrics and what's fashionable for inseams. And, designers forgive me, but their hubris is exhausting."

"Oh mercy, Haley. You are a riot! Though, I admit the fashion crowd can be a tiresome lot. A mute mannequin wearing extravagant clothing is often preferable to the verbose creators who tend to prattle on."

Nanny Green arrived with little Rosa on her hip, and Haley was happy to end the discussion about clothes. She was satisfied if what she wore was clean, in good condition, and easy to move about in. She'd never understood the obsession society had with looks. And if it weren't for Ginger, she would judge them all the same.

At first blush, the current Mrs. Reed appeared to be as shallow as the rest, with perfect hair and make-up and the latest in *haute couture*, a giggling expert in small talk. Yet, Ginger had proven Haley wrong. She was much more than what she wore, more than what a person would expect from first impressions. Ginger was one of the most intelligent people Haley knew, and that was saying a lot since Haley almost exclusively spent her time with brilliant people. On more than one occasion, Ginger had astounded Haley with her bravery, and her beautiful friend had quite a set of extraordinary and unusual skills. Ginger tended to be tight-lipped about where she'd learned them.

Once Ginger had snuggled with her daughter and the nanny had taken her back upstairs, Haley suggested they move into the parlour where they could speak freely. "Inspector Tremblay wasn't wrong about one thing," she said. "It is nice to enjoy a nightcap without fearing a Prohibition agent might knock on your door and drag you to jail."

"I can't believe it's still going on," Ginger said as they crossed the villa to the parlour. "How long do you think it will last?"

"Years," Haley said. "If not forever. The powers that be are very determined."

Ginger poured them each a small crystal glass of brandy, and they settled in as they used to at Hartigan House. One of the maids had started a fire in the room, adding to its comforting appeal.

"So, what's your opinion about our dear Inspector Tremblay?" Ginger asked.

By the twist of her rosebud lips and the glint in her green eyes, Haley could guess her friend's opinion was less than stellar. "I think he means well," Haley said, "but clearly, he doesn't understand the asset he has in you."

"Or you," Ginger said. "The two of us teaming up again on a case is delightful. Do you remember the last one?"

"Of course. Three years ago, the death at the vicar's wedding. How are Reverend and Mrs. Hill?"

"They are as happy as peaches in a pie," Ginger said, then more soberly, added, "I was in a dreadfully sour mood for weeks after you went back to Boston. But I understand, of course. No breakthroughs on your brother's murder?"

Haley shook her head. The sorrow of losing her dearest brother was always close to the surface. "One day," she said half-heartedly. Logic told her that the more time passed, the less likely it was that her brother's killer would be caught, but hope remained.

"I believe it too," Ginger said.

"But back to this case," Haley started. "How was it that no one saw Sabine Chapdelaine wander off alone? That no one noticed she had left the party?"

"That is an excellent question," Ginger said. "And one I'm eager to ask her companion at the party."

"Monsieur Bernard," Haley said.

The way Ginger stared back over the rim of her glass before taking a drink made Haley pause. "Do you know the gentleman?" she asked.

"We've met," Ginger admitted, "but long ago. I was rather surprised to see him again. I honestly didn't recognise him at first."

"Those kinds of encounters can be disconcerting," Haley said. She'd felt the same way when she'd met Ginger in Boston after first becoming acquainted in France during the war. She kept her attention on Ginger, "Do you have reason to suspect Roger Bernard could've held ill will against Madame Chapdelaine?"

"Nothing of note," Ginger said. "He seemed a perfect gentleman and rather unconcerned by the male attention his date was receiving."

"I would say that is reason to suspect ill will," Haley said. "Suppressed jealously."

"It could be," Ginger said, reconsidering. "That would make me most interested in speaking with him again. I'm quite sure the police will have done so by now."

"The husband or boyfriend is always the first to be suspected," Haley said. "What happened to Monsieur Chapdelaine?"

"They divorced last year," Ginger said.

"Could he be the culprit?" Haley pushed a lock of curls behind her ear. "It was dark enough for an intruder to enter the garden."

"Yes, but he'd have had to get her into the pool room, which is unlikely. Besides, he died of a heart attack in the spring."

Haley smirked. "I guess he's out, then. So, who does that leave us with?"

"The Rocheforts and the Millers," Ginger said.

"And Monsieur Bernard."

"Yes, him."

A tap on the door brought their conversation to a halt.

"Come in," Ginger said.

Cosette appeared, bobbed, then said, "There's a telephone call for you, Madame Reed."

"Oh," Ginger said brightly. "Is it Mr. Reed?"

"No, madame. It's Monsieur Bernard."

Haley shot Ginger a look, marvelling at how speaking of the man had conjured him up. "You're going to take the call." It was a statement rather than a question.

Ginger was already on her feet. "Of course. Please excuse me."

As Haley waited, she stoked the fire, finished her drink, and returned the empty crystal glass to the sideboard. She stared out the window, which faced the garden where the party had been held. Although it was now a vacant tidy lawn with trimmed flower gardens and hedges, Haley's mind filled the space with the party scene. Mme Chapdelaine had been the life of the party, the light that attracted the bugs, a personality that demanded attention and got it. Haley could imagine her standing by the drinks trolley, a fresh cocktail in hand, laughing through a wide mouth painted a glossy red. The men had exuded peacock-like confidence, and the women tittered with fake admiration. No wonder Haley had been eager to leave. Talk about being a square peg in a round hole. She'd had more in common with young Scout chasing Boss about the lawns and catching dragonflies than with this crowd.

Only Basil and Charles had seemed unaffected by the fashion designer, though both seemed watchful. When Ambrosia had professed fatigue and Ginger had taken her upstairs, Haley had asked Beaufort to ring for a taxicab. Being the first to leave, she hadn't seen the rest of the party leave.

Haley was so deep in thought she startled when Ginger entered the parlour. Recovering, she asked, "What did Monsieur Bernard want?"

Ginger flopped onto an armchair and crossed her legs like a dancer. "He asked me out for dinner tomorrow."

"Really?" Haley lowered herself onto the sofa. "What did you say?"

"I told him I was free for lunch."

"I doubt your husband will be happy about that," Haley said.

Ginger cocked her head. "Do you think I should've said no?"

"Oh, absolutely not," Haley said. "It's a perfect opportunity to interview him." She smiled at her friend. "I'd love to be a bug on the wall."

"Not to worry," Ginger returned. "I'll be sure to give you a full report."

11

A telegram from Basil arrived the next morning. Ginger had been preparing for her lunch appointment with M. Bernard—the man Ginger would always think of as Louis. She selected a black-and-gold tweed dress suit created by Coco Chanel. Its solid-gold bodice and matching gold scarf gave her a matronly appearance, and nothing about it could be interpreted as seductive or flirtatious.

Ginger sat on one of the armchairs in her bedroom, unfolded the telegram, and read:

Darling Ginger, we've all arrived safely. Felicia is unwell but says not to worry.

A heated ribbon of anxiety wormed through Ginger's chest at the warning to not worry. For a moment, she wondered if she should just pack up and go home, but then, she had promised Felicia a thorough recounting of the fashion parade, and Felicia would be upset if Ginger changed plans on her account.

No, if Felicia were in real trouble, this telegram would implore her to return immediately. Ginger read the rest of the telegram.

Miss you. Leave the case to the police. Please stay safe. Basil.

Ginger hummed at Basil's suggestion to leave the case to the police. She was quite certain he'd think differently had he met Inspector Tremblay in person.

Finding a pencil and pad of paper, Ginger prepared to reply. If Inspector Tremblay hadn't accused Haley, perhaps Ginger could've let the mystery of Mme Chapdelaine's death to the *Sûreté*. And it might be that she'd be forced to, as Ginger had every intention of returning to London after the fashion event ended.

Dearest Basil,

All is well here. I will endeavour to stay out of trouble. Please give my love to Scout and especially to Felicia. If her fortunes change, do let me know at once.

Yours, Ginger.

Ginger folded the paper and carried it with her

as she headed downstairs in search of Beaufort. After finding him in the kitchen, she requested that he ring for a taxicab for her, and deliver her message to the telegraph office and send it.

"*Certainement, madame,*" he said with a bow.

Though Louis had offered to pick her up, Ginger had insisted on meeting him at an outdoor café. Outdoors because it was less likely that their conversation would be overheard, and in a café, so the meeting would appear casual.

It was a pleasant drive down boulevard Raspail to the intersection of rue Delambre and boulevard du Montparnasse, where the popular Le Dôme Café was located.

The outdoor seating area was full, so it took a moment before Ginger spotted Louis at a back table. He wore a single-breasted suit with a striped tie, and his hat sat on his lap. He sat facing the street—a habit Ginger had adopted. She liked to know who was coming and going, especially if they were headed in her direction.

He rose when she drew close and kissed her as the French do, quickly on both cheeks. "*Ma chérie, you are exquisite.*"

Hobbling, Louis pulled out Ginger's chair and pushed it towards the table as she sat. He limped back to his seat and smiled over a subtle wince as he lowered himself back down.

"*Merci*, Monsieur Bernard," Ginger said, then added, "Your leg troubles you?"

Louis grinned. "Like an annoying uncle."

"This is a popular place," Ginger said.

"*Oui*. It is adored by artists and writers who love to gossip, complain, and make deals with their agents. It has come alive since the war. In fact . . " He discreetly pointed to a couple sitting three tables down. "I believe that is Ernest Hemingway with a lady that is not his wife."

Ginger peeked out from under the brim of her hat. She had read that the American writer and his wife had made Paris their home. It seemed Mrs. Hemingway was in for some heartache.

"And by the door," Louis continued, "the gentleman seated alone? That is Pablo Picasso. Have you heard of him?"

"Of course," Ginger said. "I've seen samples of his work in the magazines. A master of neoclassicism. I didn't know he lived in Paris."

"My understanding is he's the restless sort and likes to roam about Europe."

A waiter, clad in a black uniform, came to take their order. After he suggested oysters, Ginger and

Louis chose the dish along with a glass of Chardonnay. When he had gone, Louis glanced about, then lowered his voice, "It is fantastic to see you again, *Mademoiselle LaFleur*."

"Shh," Ginger said, half teasingly. "That mademoiselle died in the war."

"And a beautiful phoenix has risen from the ashes. You, *ma chérie*, have aged like fine wine."

"You are being generous, Monsieur Bernard."

"Indeed, I am not. And you must call me Roger."

"I think of you as Louis," Ginger said, "but I will continue to call you Monsieur Bernard."

Louis feigned a deep sigh. "As you wish."

Their wine arrived, and after a sip, Ginger said, "You've changed rather dramatically. When were you wounded?"

"The summer of eighteen," Louis said. "The war was hell. No room for happiness. No room for hope. The *joie de vivre* was squashed!" He smashed his fist into his palm for emphasis. "But," he continued with another sigh, "the living must go on living."

"Indeed," Ginger said. "So, how is life for you now, Monsieur Bernard?"

Louis grinned. "Well, I am still French. You, apparently, are not."

Ginger laughed and placed a palm on her chest. "I'm French in my heart."

Over their meal—and she had to admit that the briny oysters and the slices of crusty sourdough bread were divine—Ginger shared about her life in London and her family, boasting about her son and daughter. "They are an unexpected joy," she said. "I really didn't think I'd know the blessing of motherhood."

"I have no children," Louis said, "but I'm satisfied." His eyes glimmered with expectation. "And I'm free this afternoon." He paused, then added, "If you are."

"Monsieur Bernard!" Ginger said, affronted by the suggestiveness of her lunch companion. "You know that I'm married."

Louis shrugged. "As am I. This is France. Though I am without children, my wife and mistress keep me busy."

Ginger raised a brow. "Surely, you mean *'kept* you busy' in the case of your former mistress."

"*Oui, je suis désolé.*" Louis' face crumpled. "It is difficult to believe that one so vibrant and beautiful is gone."

"Tell me, Monsieur Bernard." Ginger leaned in. "How is it that you arrived at a party with the lovely

Madame Chapdelaine on your arm, but did not leave with her? That seems rather—"

"Inconsiderate?"

Calculated was the word Ginger had intended but she conceded. "Yes. Inconsiderate."

Louis leaned back. "It was her decision. She told me she'd decided to stay. I assumed you had invited her to stay the night."

"Did you tell the police that?"

"Of course," Louis returned smugly. "One must never lie to the police."

No wonder Inspector Tremblay had treated her with such suspicion. He thought she'd invited Mme Chapdelaine to stay the night. But then why hadn't the inspector asked her about that specifically? Was he gathering evidence, hoping to catch her in a lie?

Louis' eyes narrowed as he considered her. "You think I killed her, don't you?"

"Did you?"

"No. I did not. Did you?"

"Of course not. I don't have a motive."

"But you think I do."

Ginger lifted a shoulder. "She was your mistress. And she attracted the attention of a lot of men; that much was clear. Perhaps you were overcome with jealousy."

"So, I poisoned her drink."

It was Ginger's turn to narrow her eyes. "What makes you think that was the cause of death?"

"The papers say she was found in your swimming pool. I happen to know that Sabine could swim. She must have been poisoned unless she was hit over the head."

Louis was chosen to work in special operations in the field during the Great War for a reason. He was intelligent and a chameleon. He could be whatever the job required: quiet and unobtrusive or gregarious and charismatic.

"Or," he continued, "she could have been very drunk."

Ginger didn't react. She knew the official cause of death because of her friendship with Haley, but it hadn't been made public yet.

When Ginger didn't answer, Louis leaned in and chuckled. "Madame Reed, you and I are on the same side. We are allies."

"The war is over, Monsieur Bernard," Ginger said. "I'm on the side of truth."

Louis leaned back, his gaze growing serious. After a long pause, he said, "I worried about you that night. I wanted to help you, but I was—"

"Your oath bound you," Ginger said. "I understand." She flung her arms out wide. "And I escaped, unharmed."

"Yes," Louis said. "Your escape was all that was talked about by the English and the Germans, and the blame was, er, misdirected."

"What do you mean?"

"Someone had to pay for your betrayal that night, *ma chérie.*"

Ginger's skin tingled. Who had paid? Not Louis. He said his leg injury happened later the next summer. The party they'd worked on, both of them as spies listening in on the conversations of important German commanders, had taken place on New Year's Eve. "Who?" she asked softly. "Who was blamed?"

"It is not important." Louis rubbed his palms together. "What was done was done. We must, all of us, move on."

The waiter strolled by, and Ginger waved her hand for the bill. "*Excusez-moi, garçon. L'addition, s'il vous plaît.*"

"*Non,*" Louis said as the bill was delivered. "I invited you, Madame Reed. Please allow me to pay."

Ginger wanted to avoid any appearance of their meeting being anything but platonic but relented to avoid a scene. "*Merci, monsieur.*"

Louis walked with his staggering gait alongside Ginger, between the tables of the other customers on the patio, to the road. He paused and ducked his chin. "Forgive me, madame. I did not mean to offend an old friend."

Ginger flashed a quick smile, but her attention was captured by a couple seated inside the café at the window. How serendipitous to cross paths in this way!

"Madame?"

"None was taken, Monsieur Bernard," Ginger said, returning her focus to her old ally. "It was a pleasure to become reacquainted, and perhaps we will run into each other again before I leave Paris."

"I would like that very much."

Ginger let out a small huff. Her politeness wasn't intended to offer the Frenchman hope of a rendezvous. She had to watch what she said to ensure her words couldn't be mistaken for a double entendre.

"Would you mind if we part ways here?" she said. "I would like to visit the ladies' before I leave."

"Certainly, madame." Louis bowed as he took her hand and kissed it. Ginger was glad she'd taken the time to put her gloves back on.

Pivoting on the heels of her T-strap shoes,

Ginger entered the café as if she were a new patron just arriving. She walked past the Millers' table, then feigned astonishment.

"Mr. and Mrs. Miller! How are you? Allow me to extend my condolences. I didn't know Madame Chapdelaine was your sister, madame, until recently."

Mrs. Miller, a lady moving away from the perfection of youth but not quite crossed over to the faded beauty of the aged, pressed a ready handkerchief under heavily made-up eyes. "*C'est incroyable!* And we only just arrived to see her!"

Mr. Miller, sporting dark circles under his eyes, motioned to the empty chair. "Would you join us, Madame Reed?"

"Oh, I wouldn't want to intrude," Ginger said, hoping the invitation would become emphatic. She was rewarded.

"We insist," Mr. Miller said, then to his bereaved wife, "Don't we, dear?"

Mrs. Miller nodded. "Perhaps you could answer our questions. The police are being impossible."

Ginger took the proffered chair. "I'd be happy to answer any questions I can" she replied.

The Millers had finished their meal and were drinking coffee. Ginger ordered a cup of her own.

"There's no one who makes coffee better than the French," she said amiably.

Mrs. Miller's eyes lit up. "I could not agree more. Do you know Americans like to drink *instant* coffee?"

Ginger chuckled. "I do. I lived in Boston for many years."

"Ah," Mrs. Miller said with a note of camaraderie. "Then you do know."

Ginger took a sip of coffee, and when a question wasn't immediately forthcoming, she asked one of her own. "Were you and your sister close, Madame Miller?"

Aurélie Miller hesitated. "We were closer when we were younger. But then I married Brian and moved to New York, and she . . ."

Ginger ventured, "She became a fashion celebrity?"

"*Oui,*" she said simply.

"I'm not one for gossip," Ginger started, "but in light of the tragedy, I did ask my staff if they heard or saw anything of note . . ."

"And?" Brian Miller said with a hint of impatience.

"Well, I'll try to be delicate, but Sabine Chapdelaine seemed to be a magnet for the opposite sex. I witnessed it myself at my garden party."

Mr. Miller's eyes flashed with guilt as he looked away, as if he knew he was amongst those to whom Ginger referred, and hurriedly drew his coffee cup to his lips.

Ginger continued, "You, Mrs. Miller, were overheard referring to your sister as a wolf."

"That was meaningless," Mrs. Miller said with a flick of her wrist. "Simple sibling rivalry. You saw her, Mrs. Reed. She was so drunk she could barely stand up, much less hold her tongue. It was hardly a moment of familial pride."

Ginger leaned back, taking her turn to drink her coffee, thinking how the sister's display of grief had quickly turned to disdain. Had she come back to France to dispatch her sister? With Mme Chapdelaine's husband deceased, and no children, Mrs. Miller was the lady's direct heir.

Setting her coffee cup on the table, she said, "Was there something you wanted to ask me?"

Mrs. Miller reached for Ginger's hand. "Did you see . . . her? Do you know what happened?"

"I was there shortly after the body was discovered," Ginger said gently. "My maid, Lizzie, was the one to find her. The police came shortly afterwards, and the investigation is ongoing. I'm afraid I don't know what happened."

Mr. Miller paid for their meals and included the cost of Ginger's coffee.

"Thank you," Ginger said as she got to her feet. "It was good to see you again, though I wish the circumstances were different."

"As do we," Mr. Miller said.

Ginger joined them as they walked out the door and onto the pavement; before they went their separate ways, she said, "Oh, I suppose you will be the ones to inherit Madame Chapdelaine's estate? She was known to be quite wealthy."

The Millers stared back with stunned expressions, Mrs. Miller blanching and Mr. Miller's neck flashing crimson. "We've not even had time to think of such things," Mr. Miller said sharply.

"Of course," Ginger said. "Forgive me. I do hope all goes well for you."

The Millers left in a huff as Ginger walked in the opposite direction towards a waiting taxicab. She'd known her comment would be construed as rude when she said it, but the couple's reaction was telling. Were they the type who would kill for money?

12

*H*aley was surprised to discover that after her practicum hours at the hospital, she'd returned to the villa before Ginger. As she changed her clothes—something she always did after time spent in the mortuary—she wondered if the luncheon with Louis had gone fantastically well or terribly wrong. She pushed down a bubble of worry in her gut. Ginger was resourceful and well versed in self-preservation techniques. It was the middle of the day, and she was in a busy, crowded city where a scream from a beautiful lady would attract attention. Likely, Ginger's attention had been captured by one of many dress shops, both glitzy and sophisticated, in a way that could rival her Feathers & Flair shop back in England.

Having washed her face, tamed her curls into a knot at the back of her head, and donned clean trousers and a button-down blouse, Haley headed down the staircase towards the kitchen. She hadn't eaten since breakfast, and her stomach was complaining. Though she could've rung a bell, Haley hadn't been raised with servants waiting on her hand and foot and felt more comfortable rummaging through the kitchen cupboards and refrigerator on her own, presuming she found the kitchen empty.

Which she did not. In fact, the heavenly smell of freshly baked bread lured her inside, despite the two occupants who stared back in question on seeing her standing in the doorway.

"Pardon me," Haley said. "But that bread smells amazing."

Mme Dupris wiped her hands on her apron. "Would you like a slice, Mademoiselle 'Iggins?"

Haley pursed her lips to stop grinning. Her name was a challenge for the French, with her first and last name starting with the letter *H*—traditionally silent in the French language. She didn't know if she'd ever grow accustomed to being called 'Aley 'Iggins.

The cook added, "I've got fresh butter and a new, opened jar of preserves."

"That would be fabulous," Haley said. Though she hadn't been invited to, she took a seat at the rudimentary wooden table in the room.

The maid, Cosette, was also in the kitchen and did the actual slicing of the bread.

"Making bread is one of my favourite things to do," she said in good but strongly accented English. "How the wheat works with the water, salt, and yeast when they are mixed together. A small round of dough grows through fermentation."

The girl brought her a thick slice of bread, spread generously with butter and jam.

Not wanting to stay in the way of two hard-working women, Haley picked up her plate. "I'll just take this to my room."

"If that is what you like, mademoiselle," Cosette said. She offered a slight curtsey, then went to the kitchen sink where a pile of bread pans and dirty dishes waited to be washed.

As soon as Haley was out of the kitchen, she took a bite of the bread and nearly moaned out loud. The crunchy crust, melt-in-your-mouth airy bread, farm-fresh butter, and jam almost made her knees weak. Nothing satisfied an empty stomach better!

There was no way this slice wouldn't be

consumed before she even made it to her bedroom, so instead of heading up the stairs, she took the hallway that led to the back garden. The slice of bread was half gone by the time she reached the pool room, where she stopped, stared through the glass, and recalled the body found there the day before. For some people, the memory of a dead and bloated body would interfere with their appetite, but not Haley. She easily finished the bread and licked her fingers without an iota of queasiness.

Unsure what to do with her empty plate, she took it into the pool room and set it on the table. She'd return it to the kitchen on her way out, but for the moment, she wanted to sit and think. After wiping her hands on her trousers, she tugged at the fabric before taking a chair. Staring at the water, Haley noted it was beginning to turn green. A decomposing body would upset the pH . The pool would have to be drained and refilled before anyone could swim in it again.

Her mind returned to the decomposing body. Mme Chapdelaine had ingested chloroform, but when? Before she entered the pool room or after? Had she wandered in alone, or had someone enticed her there? Why hadn't anyone noticed . . . particularly Roger Bernard? Haley was sure Ginger would have the answer to that question by now.

She checked her watch. It was nearly five o'clock. Dinner was served late in France, but surely Ginger would be home long before then as she didn't like to spend too much time away from little Rosa.

"If she's not back in an hour, I'll start a search," she said aloud, her voice echoing slightly in the cavernous room.

The Rocheforts were from a class of people who lived in hotel suites. Ginger was acquainted with several like them in London who lived in suites at the Ritz, the Savoy, or Brown's Hotel during the cooler months and summered in their usually lavish country properties. Like Mme Chapdelaine, the Rocheforts were fashion celebrities, if on a slightly lower rung, and much of their lives was splashed about in the society pages. Though, and Ginger knew this from experience, most of what one read there had to be taken with a grain of salt. The truth was usually watered down if it existed at all.

If one was to go by what one read, and Ginger did keep up with the gossip, Gaspard and Bérénice Rochefort were on the verge of a divorce and sleeping in separate bedrooms. And even worse, Gaspard had a different mistress every day of the week.

If Ginger were to guess, the first half of that scenario might be true. Still, Gaspard Rochefort didn't seem energetic enough to keep up with such a tight calendar of love affairs, nor was he the sort of individual who naturally caught a woman's eye. Ginger also knew that certain celebrity types moved from address to address to avoid excessive publicity, but the last she'd heard, the couple were residing at the Hôtel Ronceray. With the fashion parade coming up, they were probably eager for any publicity, and chances were good they hadn't moved in the last day.

The Hôtel Ronceray was in Montmartre, the wide white building towering over the Passage Jouffroy, the old covered shopping arcade on the boulevard Montmartre.

As Ginger pulled to the kerb across the street, she spotted the Rocheforts approaching the hotel. She'd paid the driver, then raised her hand as she called across the busy road. "Monsieur Rochefort! Madame Rochefort!"

The couple glanced her way and then quickly turned their heads. Mme Rochefort gripped her husband's arm as he pulled her into the arched doorway that led into the Passage Jouffroy to get to the doors of the Hôtel Ronceray.

Drat! Ginger was sure they had seen her. Clearly, they weren't in the mood to speak to her. Undaunted, Ginger crossed the road when a break in traffic presented itself and headed inside.

She approached the reception desk in the lobby, which was richly fashioned in dark wood and emerald greens. "Please inform the Rocheforts that Mrs. Reed is here to see them," she said in French.

The fellow kept his expression blank, a skill that Ginger respected as she knew it took some training to master, and told her the Rocheforts weren't accepting visitors that day. "They regret that they are busy getting ready for the show tomorrow. You understand?"

Ginger understood completely. The Rocheforts didn't want to speak to her. But why? Had Inspector Tremblay warned them away? Or were they afraid of the questions she might pose?

Either way, Ginger could hardly demand an audience, and making a scene would be useless.

"*Merci*," she said politely, then smiled before turning away. The Rocheforts couldn't avoid her forever. She would see them at the fashion parade.

There was nothing left to do but head back to the

villa. She longed to hold little Rosa, and she'd promised Basil and Scout she would write at least once during the week. And Haley would be there soon as well.

Ginger hailed another taxicab and gave the address of the villa. She was tempted to close her eyes and rest them on the way back, but she was in Paris, and who knew when she would return? She didn't want to miss a moment, so she decided to take in the sights.

The taxi took her down the boulevard des Italiens, leaving the ornate building of the Palais Garnier on their right as they crossed the Place de l'Opéra. Ginger craned her neck to look up at the façade of the Madeleine Church that looked more like a Grecian temple than anything else, then peered out the front window of the taxi as it turned left onto rue Royale and drove straight towards the obelisk on the Place de la Concorde. Ginger shuddered as she remembered how this had been the bloody site of "Madame la Guillotine" in the French Revolution, and she was glad when they turned to roll up the broad stretch of the Champs-Élysées. The sight of the Louis Vuitton shop gave her a twinge of regret—she would not be able to stop for a new handbag this time as she had planned, but the case took priority.

She looked out the left window of the taxi as it rounded the Arc de Triomphe. No matter how often she saw the majestic monument, it never failed to impress her with its sheer size and grandeur. The flame on the Tomb of the Unknown Soldier beneath the grand arch was lit, as it had been since that one nameless fighter had been interred there in 1920, and Ginger could not help but wonder if, perhaps, the man who lay there representing all the fallen was one of her friends lost in the war.

Ginger was still musing on how well Paris had recovered from the ravages of the war when the taxicab drew near to the villa, and she spotted a familiar form scurrying down the pavement. The blonde hair tucked under a plain cloche hat and the long neck bending forward was clearly the maid Elise.

Where was she off to in such a hurry?

The maid stopped suddenly, hesitated for a moment, then entered a corner establishment. As the taxicab driver turned a corner, Ginger caught the name. La Petite Porte Rouge.

That was the bar where Denis Faucher worked, the barman who hadn't made it to Ginger's garden party due to sudden illness. Perhaps that was why Elise was calling in? To check on the man's health?

Or perhaps she was late for a shift. Beaufort had said that the villa staff worked in other jobs as well. It was possible that Elise was simply showing up to work.

13

Galeries Lafayette was an architectural work of art, with its domed glass ceiling, ornate gold-and-red pillars, and three-tiered rows of seating that looked down on an open hall where the fashion parade would take place. Anticipation filled the place with low conversations echoing like waves. Ginger had brought Haley as her guest, and they sat in the front row, a prestigious placement due to Ginger's connection with the late Mme Chapdelaine.

For the occasion, Ginger had selected a delicate emerald-green evening gown with thin straps and a low-cut back. A sequinned headpiece sat on her hair like a headband, a long strand of pearls fell from her neck, and teardrop earrings swung playfully from her ears as she walked. Somewhat reluctantly, Haley wore a gown chosen by Ginger—a flowy chiffon with a pale blue and red floral pattern.

"I'm only here because of the case," Haley mumbled.

"As you've mentioned," Ginger said with a smirk. "More than once."

"It needs to be said." She patted a small black doctor's bag by her feet. "And just in case. There *is* a killer on the loose."

"I'm just glad Dr. Lyon allowed you the time off," Ginger stated.

"I was due a few hours."

Ginger played with her pearl rope-necklace as she considered her friend. Haley spent most of her time studying and working on her practicum. Ginger had suffered a touch of envy and regret that Haley couldn't spend more time with herself and her family when they were simultaneously in Paris. The silver lining, in this case, was that it had brought the two together in a more concentrated way.

Like old times.

"I only hope it's worth my while," Haley said. "Not that being here with you isn't lovely, but I don't want to embarrass you by falling asleep."

Ginger rolled her eyes. "I guarantee that the spectacle on the runway will keep your senses stimulated."

Haley hummed noncommittally.

"I'd like to corner the Rocheforts somehow." Ginger had explained to Haley how the fashion couple had shunned her the afternoon before. "Clearly, they have something to hide."

"They are why I eventually agreed to join you here today," Haley replied.

People bustled in and out of a door next to the runway. Ginger knew a lot of activity happened behind the scenes with designers' assistants organising the live mannequins and delivering frocks and gowns for them to wear on the runway. Waiters and waitresses scurried to keep the crowd happy as the spectators waited.

Was that Cosette? Ginger craned her neck, but the maid had turned and disappeared. In her maid's outfit, Cosette could easily be mistaken for another. Besides, Ginger was pretty certain Cosette had been in the kitchen assisting Mme Dupris when she had left the villa.

But the waiter carrying a tray of champagne was most certainly Beaufort. When he saw them, he smiled softly. "Madame Reed, Mademoiselle 'Iggins.

Would you care for champagne?

"Thank you, Beaufort," Ginger said.

Haley also extended her gratitude, and they sipped the tart, bubbly drink with pleasure.

Haley pointed. "There they are."

Ginger followed the direction of her pinkie and found the target. M. and Mme Rochefort were overseeing their assistants, giving terse instructions.

"They look swamped," Haley said.

"Perfect," Ginger returned as she got to her feet. "They won't have time to think through their responses." She gazed down at Haley. "Are you coming?"

Haley smoothed out her dress as she stood. "Right behind you."

Mme Rochefort spotted them before her husband did, making no attempt to conceal a scowl. Ginger responded in the opposite spirit, smiling broadly and greeting the couple enthusiastically.

"Madame Rochefort, Monsieur! Such a pleasure to see you again. I am looking forward to seeing your autumn line today. So much fun! Oh, you remember my American friend, Mademoiselle Higgins?" Ginger pulled Haley into the huddle. "From my party the other night?"

The Rocheforts nodded stiffly. "Of course," M.

Rochefort said. "How could we forget anything about that night."

Ginger let her features fall. "*Bien sûr*. Such a tragedy. You must miss your friend deeply, especially today; God bless her soul."

"Madame Chapedelaine was a force to be reckoned with in the fashion world," Mme Rochefort said.

"Rather strong competition, I suspect," Haley added.

The Rocheforts glared at her as if she were a servant who didn't know her place. Haley was undaunted, and Ginger watched with admiration as her friend continued.

"With her out of the running today, you have the esteemed place of opening and closing the show."

"I'm not sure what you're driving at, mademoiselle," M. Rochefort said, staying in motion as he examined the frocks and gowns hanging on the rod. "I deny being threatened by Madame Chapdelaine's designs. But, as you stated, we have an important show and are too busy right now for chit-chat."

"But she's not wrong," Ginger said. She set her glass down on a nearby table to secure a loose lock of hair and adjust her hat. "And I've been told that you,

Madame Rochefort, said that fashion wasn't the only prize Madame Chapdelaine was after."

The lady in question glared. "I do not know what you mean."

Ginger stepped in closer and lowered her voice. "I've heard that perhaps Monsieur Bernard wasn't Madame Chapdelaine's only lover." Ginger hadn't heard this, but it wasn't beyond the realm of possibility. She waited to see how the couple responded. "Jealousy can drive one to do something one later regrets."

"That is not true!" Mme Rochefort said sharply. "Gaspard despised the woman."

"Enough to kill her?"

Gaspard Rochefort threw his palms open. "Madame Reed, I protest. You are barking up the wrong tree. Perhaps you should be looking at Brian Miller."

Bérénice Rochefort gave her husband a sour look but said nothing. She moved about the rack of clothing like a bee investigating a bouquet, buzzing about with her back to Ginger and Haley. She gave a distinct impression that she'd like to sting them if they didn't leave her alone.

Ginger shared a look with Haley, then asked, "Why should we consider Mr. Miller?"

"The only reason Monsieur Miller returned to France," M. Rochefort said stiffly, "was because he was going bankrupt. He wanted his wife to ask her sister for money."

"And how do you know this?" Haley asked.

"Aurélie Miller and I are friendly," Mme Rochefort said. She'd been milling about but had stayed close enough to hear. "She confided in me. Now—" The lady stilled and placed her hands on her hips. "Unless you are in the company of the police, we will not allow you to subject us to further accusations."

Ginger picked up her glass of champagne as the two designers stormed behind the curtain and out of view.

"That went well," Haley said, taking a sip of her champagne.

Ginger took a drink as well. "Better than I expected, actually." She linked arms with Haley and started towards their seats in the front row.

They didn't quite make it before Ginger was gripped with searing abdominal pain.

"Ginger!" Haley said, tightening her grip on Ginger's arm. "What's the matter? Are you all right?"

Ginger glanced at her friend, wincing as another

pain gripped her. The last thing she remembered before blacking out was the crash of her glass hitting the floor and dangerously sharp shards scattering everywhere.

14

On reflex, Haley grabbed Ginger's arm before her mind even registered what was happening, effectively preventing a dangerous crack of Ginger's beautiful head. She also pulled Ginger's falling body away from the most dangerous pieces of broken glass.

"Ginger!" Haley hovered over her friend with growing alarm as she watched Ginger's lips turn a shade of blue despite the red lipstick coating them. Lowering her ear to the lips, Haley held her breath, only exhaling when she determined that Ginger was still breathing. Two fingers on Ginger's porcelain neck confirmed a weakened pulse.

"We need an ambulance!" Haley shouted, then again in French. "*Appelez une ambulance!*" Haley wasn't as fluent in French as Ginger was, but she knew enough French to follow her lectures, and her medical terminology was in order.

Haley removed the pearls Ginger wore, then stroked the red strands of hair off her face. "Stay with us, Ginger. Help is on the way."

A crowd had gathered, and a familiar form broke through the ranks, the footman Beaufort.

"Madame Reed!" he said with a start. Then to Haley, "What is wrong with her?" He spoke French, but his meaning would've been clear if he'd been speaking a primitive African tongue.

Haley shook her head. *Did someone poison her? But how?* Ginger had been with her the whole evening, and Haley herself was fine. They had had nothing to eat and the champagne Beaufort had delivered to them was their only drink. She stared at the footman working as a waiter with eyes of suspicion. How prudent to be so close to the scene and amongst the first to show concern.

Taking a whiff of Ginger's shallow breath, Haley detected notes of bitter almonds through the tartness of the champagne. *Cyanide?*

"Beaufort, get me my black bag." The footman-turned-waiter gave her a perplexed stare.

"Quickly!" Haley pointed to her chair, where the

bag sat on the floor, and the man hurried to do her bidding, delivering the bag in short order. While Beaufort was busy doing that, Haley commanded a maid to bring her a glass of water and another of lemonade—an offer for those who didn't want to drink alcohol—and to ask another maid to find a bit of washing soda, commonly used to spot clean fashion garments.

Haley kept a small jar of iron supplements in her black bag. She broke a capsule into the lemonade and mixed the washing soda into the water. Together they were known as Solutions A and B and were known to neutralise the effects of cyanide poisoning.

Haley coaxed Ginger to drink each glass, one at a time. Ginger responded with a gag reflex, but Haley stroked her neck to encourage swallowing, and most of the concoctions were consumed.

Haley turned back to the footman who had remained, watching. "Beaufort," she began, "please put on your gloves, then pick up this glass." She pointed at the shards of Ginger's champagne glass. "Put it into a cloth napkin. Carefully, now. It's evidence for the police."

Haley watched to ensure Beaufort did exactly as instructed, and when he was done, she took the wrapped glass pieces from him.

Time seemed to stop as she waited for the ambulance. The Rocheforts returned from whatever fashion abyss they'd fallen into.

Mme Rochefort's gloved hand covered her mouth. "*Mon Dieu.* Has she fainted? Is she all right?" She waved her arm, and one of her assistants came running. "Get the smelling salts."

To Haley's relief, Ginger moaned, and her thick eyelashes flickered. "Haley?"

Her breathing was strained and her voice shallow, but Haley couldn't remember a time the sound of her name from the lips of another had brought her so much joy.

"Yes, Ginger, I'm here. Now don't speak. Save your energy. The ambulance is on the way."

The fact that Ginger didn't protest or raise herself on her elbows was a testament to the seriousness of her condition. She hadn't simply fainted.

With relief, Haley stood back when the ambulance attendants arrived and hovered as they lifted Ginger onto the gurney. The crowd of the curious closed ranks behind them, their eyes focusing back on the tantalising catwalk of the models wearing this season's fall line. Ginger Reed was merely a foreigner, and she hadn't died, so apparently, there was no reason to fuss.

"Can I ride with you?" Haley asked. Then added, "I'm a medical student working at the hospital."

The attendant shrugged and offered Haley assistance into the back of the van, which she didn't need, but graciously accepted. As she sat by Ginger, she hugged her doctor's bag, which contained Ginger's broken champagne glass, and then took Ginger's hand.

"We'll find out who did this," she said. "I promise. Now focus on getting well, or Basil will have my head."

Ginger didn't open her eyes, but Haley could swear the corner of her mouth pulled up in a slight smile.

It was sometime the next day when Ginger's eyes worked open. Her surroundings, a blurry white and grey, smelled not of the fresh-cut jasmine she was accustomed to but the acrid scent of antiseptic. After a few moments, her vision cleared, her mind registering awareness and answering at least one question. She was in a hospital.

Ginger took a moment to wiggle her fingers and toes, lifted her knees, and bent her elbows. Next, she carefully moved her chin from side to side and then turned her neck. Her limbs seemed uninjured, which meant she hadn't been in an accident.

So why was she there?

She attempted to call for the nurse but coughed at the effort, her voice hoarse and scratchy. At least a glass of water sat on the small table beside her bed. Carefully, she reached for it, clawed it with her fingers, and brought it to her mouth with a shaky hand as she lifted her head.

It was tepid but wet and soothed her raw throat.

It hurt to swallow.

Something had happened that had scorched her throat. She pinched her eyes shut as she tried to remember. What was the last thing she could recall?

The fashion parade! She'd been there with Haley.

Haley! Was she all right? Was she a patient in this hospital as well?

Ginger remembered she was in France and called out in French as loud as she could bear. "*Infirmière!*"

"Madame Reed."

Finally, a nurse. "Mademoiselle Higgins," Ginger sputtered. "Is she here?"

"*Oui, oui.*"

Ginger felt a surge of panic. "Is she all right? *Est-ce qu'elle va bien?*"

"*Certainement, madame.*" The nurse continued in French. "She went to get a coffee. She will be back soon."

Ginger relaxed into her pillow. Haley was getting coffee. That meant she wasn't a patient.

"Why am I here?" Ginger asked.

"You had your stomach pumped, *ma chérie.*" The nurse clucked as she adjusted Ginger's pillow and refilled her glass of water. "Now you must rest. A doctor will be in to see you shortly."

At least the nurse didn't seem overly worried about Ginger's immediate well-being, but her news explained Ginger's irritated throat. And now, since sipping the water and having her pillow fluffed, Ginger felt strong enough to put weight on her elbows and lift herself to a sitting position.

"Well, aren't you a sight for sore eyes!"

Ginger turned to Haley's voice and extended her arms for a quick embrace. "As are you," Ginger said as they hugged. "I need answers, and I need them now."

Haley pulled a wooden chair up to the side of Ginger's metal-framed bed.

"I'll do my best." She grimaced and added, "But you won't like it."

"Oh mercy. Now I'm really curious. No, let me guess." Ginger put a finger to her lips. "Someone tried to poison me."

"They don't call you Lady Gold of Lady Gold Investigations for nothing."

"The nurse said my stomach was pumped." Ginger rubbed her abdomen, acknowledging the tenderness there. "Chloroform again?"

Haley shook her head. "Cyanide. Our poisoner doesn't appear to have a favourite."

"Or they are all his favourites," Ginger retorted.

"Or that," Haley conceded. "It was slipped into your drink at the fashion parade. I tested the broken pieces of the glass myself." Haley lowered her chin, staring at Ginger with a look of gratitude. "Thankfully, you didn't drink it too quickly."

"I don't understand," Ginger said. "Why would someone poison *me*?" She stared back at Haley. "Are you sure I was the intended target?"

"That's our hypothesis."

"*Our?*"

"Mine and the police's."

"I see. What does Inspector Tremblay have to say?"

"Oh, I'm sure he'll be here to ask you all his questions soon. The nurses were instructed to let him know when you woke up."

"We'd better hurry, then," Ginger said. "Tell me what you know."

"We were both given goblets of champagne by Beaufort . . ."

"Beaufort was there?"

Haley nodded. "And the maids, Elise Cadieux and Cosette Padou. The villa doesn't give them full-time work, so they pick up other jobs when they come along."

Ginger nodded. "Ah, yes. I remember seeing them there now. And Beaufort gave us the drinks?"

"He did."

"He's also the one who gave the final cocktail to Elise to give to Sabine Chapdelaine." Ginger gave Haley a sideways glance. "So, what did he have to say for himself? Is he our poisoner?"

"It's possible, though Tremblay wouldn't allow me to sit in on any interviews," Haley said. "I wanted to be here with you anyway." She offered a smile. "But then you go and wake up the one time I leave the room."

"I'm so selfish," Ginger said dryly. "But thank you for being here."

"Of course." Haley leaned in. "Now, why would someone want to poison you?"

Ginger shook her head, perplexed. "I'm a visitor to the country. I come once or twice a year to shop for my store. I spent almost all of my time with family and you this time."

"And a few colleagues in fashion," Haley added.

"Well, yes. It would've been rude to come to Paris and not see the few friends and acquaintances I do have here."

"Perhaps the killer has a thing against redheads," Haley said. "Redheads who like fashion."

Ginger frowned. "That would be a particular fetish, to be sure."

"Beaufort is Tremblay's prime suspect," Haley said, "but I can't think of a motive for him wanting you dead."

"Nor I," Ginger said. "If Madame Chapdelaine was the intended victim, perhaps there is a history there we've yet to uncover."

"And then he moves on from her to you?" Haley said. "Maybe he gets a taste of killing and decides he likes it?"

"Stranger things have happened," Ginger said.

Haley nodded in agreement, then added, "There were others who could've tainted your drink."

Ginger agreed. "The Rocheforts. I remember how restless they were when we talked to them, shifting about, looking over my shoulder. I was careless when I lowered my glass onto the table and let it out of my sight."

That had been a novice move, and Ginger silently chastised herself. The more time that passed by from her time working as a secret service agent in the war, the more lackadaisical she'd become. Perhaps one should be able to relax during peacetime, but still. Her inattentiveness was no excuse. Such laziness would've got her killed during the war, and it had almost got her killed now.

"Again the question is why me?" Ginger said. "Unless they didn't like the fact that I was asking questions about their rival. I'm wondering if Sabine Chapdelaine and I are both intended victims. She the first, and me the second for meddling and getting too close to the truth."

"We can't rule out the maids and waiters," Haley said. "They shuffled past regularly. It turns out we were standing at the corridor's entrance to the back, just in their way."

"Elise," Ginger started. "You said she was there?"

"She was."

"I saw her two days ago. Going into La Petite Porte Rouge."

"Isn't that the pub where the barman works? The one who didn't show up for your garden party?"

"Yes. Denis Faucher. He claimed to have suddenly become ill. Too ill to come to work, which according to Mme Dupris, must've meant quite ill, as he has a large family to support."

"I suppose it wouldn't be too odd for Elise to go to Mr. Faucher's place of business."

"No," Ginger admitted. "But she seemed in rather a hurry as she walked along the pavement, but then, when she got to the door, she hesitated, as if she didn't want to go in." Ginger let out a long breath. "It's probably nothing."

"Probably not," Haley said, standing. "But I think I might go chat with Mr. Faucher as long as you feel at ease about me leaving you alone."

"Do go," Ginger said. "I'd like to know what he has to say. Besides, I don't think I'm really alone. Isn't that a police officer outside the door?" Ginger had glimpsed the man's uniform when Haley had come in.

"It is," Haley said. "I didn't want to trouble you by saying so. I'm sure you're safe here."

"I am until Tremblay corners me," Ginger said

with a grin. "Now get going before he arrives and starts asking you nosy questions."

"Yes, ma'am," Haley said, getting to her feet.

"Oh, and Haley?" Ginger started.

"Yes?"

"Thanks for saving my life."

Haley flashed her signature wide grin. "You can't always be the one doing the saving, Ginger."

15

*L*a Petite Porte Rouge was a long, narrow hole-in-the-wall establishment with exposed brick, plenty of wood, and gas lighting. And, as expected, a door painted a vibrant red. On the shelf behind the bar were open shelves with a motley collection of crystal glasses and goblets, including several blue-tinted ones that looked like the one Ginger had described. A barmaid behind the counter was busy cleaning dishes as the barman stared.

In French, he asked, "Can I help you, mademoiselle?"

In her rudimentary French, Haley answered, "Are you Monsieur Denis Faucher?"

The man's brows furrowed. "You are

American?"

Haley nodded. "My name is Higgins. I'm a medical student working at the hospital."

"I am Faucher," he returned in stilted English. "Why do you want me?"

"I'm a guest of Madame Reed, who is staying at Villa Legrand," Haley said, switching back to English. "You were supposed to attend the bar at her garden party last week."

"Oh, *oui. Je suis désolé.*" He placed a palm on his stomach. "I had a sudden *maladie.*"

"Did it come on suddenly?" Haley asked. "Or slowly over time?"

M. Faucher worked his lips. "Suddenly, *oui.* A shame. I hate to miss working." He cocked his head as he stroked a cleanly shaven face. "Why are you interested in my health, mademoiselle?"

"You must have heard about the tragedy that happened the night of the party."

The barman pushed out his lower lip as he slowly shook his head. "It was in all the newspapers. *Incroyable.* Falling into a swimming pool."

"And sadly, Madame Reed has taken ill as well."

M. Faucher settled his brown-eyed gaze on Haley. "I still don't understand."

Haley removed a folded paper from her handbag, smoothed it, and placed it on the countertop. It was a list of everyone on the premises during the party.

"Do you recognise any of these names?" she asked.

He pushed out his lip again. "*Je ne sais pas*. The name Rochefort stands out. Parisians, no?"

"They are," Haley said. "They are well known in the fashion industry."

"I have read about them in the newspapers, that is all."

"Perhaps they have frequented your establishment?"

"I doubt that. The clientele of La Petite Porte Rouge comes from the middle class and lower. No pearls and diamonds, if you know what I mean."

Haley pointed to the portion of the list containing the names of the staff working at the villa: Sophie Dupris, Elise Cadieux, Cosette Padou, Bruno Beaufort. "What about these names?"

M. Faucher shrugged. "Nothing stands out."

"What about her?" Haley pointed to Elise's name. "She was seen entering this pub two days ago."

"Plenty of people come here, mademoiselle," the barman said, frustration entering his voice. "There are some here today who need me to serve them." He rubbed his fingertips together, a gesture symbolising money.

"I'll have a sherry," Haley said, taking a seat on one of the stools. If she were going to take up so much of the man's time, she should make it worth his while.

M. Faucher nodded, turned for a glass from a shelf along the back wall, selected a sherry, poured it, and slid it in Haley's direction.

After taking a sip, Haley continued, "Elise Cadieux works at the villa. All of those people do. She's slender, with dirty-blonde hair, and slouches a little."

The barman screwed up his face. "Slouches?"

Haley stood to demonstrate.

The barman laughed. "Alas! I do not know her. All the maids look the same to me. Especially in the uniforms."

"She might have returned a blue glass?" Haley pointed to the clean ones sitting upside down on the shelf. "Like those."

M. Faucher wrinkled his nose as he pointed a stubby finger at the glasses and counted out loud. "*Un, deux, trois, quatre, cinq . . . six?*"

"You sound surprised," Haley said.

"There were only five, mademoiselle. I thought one was broken or stolen, but now, here it is."

It seemed one had been borrowed and returned. Was this why Elise had come to the pub that day? To return the glass? "Monsieur Faucher, do you recall what you ate or drank before falling ill?" Haley asked.

"For me, I eat the same food for lunch each day. A slice of quiche. I help it along with a little whisky." He shrugged. "It is my *prérogative*."

"Prerogative?"

"*Oui*. As the head barman."

"Who was with you that day?"

"The usual staff." His eyebrows jumped as he snapped his fingers. "Et, *oui*! Some people from the villa." He grinned. "They bought a lot of alcohol."

"Do you remember who?" Haley asked.

"A young man—"

"Beaufort?"

"*Oui*, I believe that was his name. And a young lady."

"Elise?"

M. Faucher shook his head and cast an apologetic look. "I don't remember." He lifted the bottle of sherry that had stayed on the counter. "Would you like more?"

"*Non, merci,*" Haley said. She dropped a few coins on the counter before leaving. "*Au revoir.*" She almost added, "Be careful," but didn't want to alarm the man. Haley didn't think he was truly in danger. He'd be dead if that were what the poisoner had intended. It had been enough for him or her to make the barman sick to prevent him from getting in the way at the party.

Haley pulled on the door just as it was being pushed from the other side, the momentum nearly knocking her over. To her amazement, Brian Miller stepped inside.

The man removed his hat. "Miss Higgins?"

"Mr. Miller." Smoothing out her skirt, she offered a slight smile. "Fancy meeting you here."

"I'm just as surprised as you," Mr. Miller said.

Haley made a show of looking behind the man. "No Mrs. Miller?"

"Uh, no. She's getting her hair done at the salon." He grinned. "She misses gossiping in the French language. I thought I'd get a drink while I waited."

Haley could hardly judge the man for imbibing so early in the day, as she'd just done so herself. She smiled at her fellow American. "Do you mind if I join you?" she asked. "It's just nice to speak English with someone and know you'll be clearly understood."

Mr. Miller's eyes flashed briefly with annoyance but then softened. Politely, he said, "I'd be delighted."

Haley took a seat on the opposite side of a small square wooden table and raised an index finger to Denis Faucher, indicating she'd have another sherry.

Mr. Miller called out, "A whisky for me, sir."

The barmaid delivered the drinks, and Mr. Miller raised his glass. "To American tourists." Haley clicked hers to his and echoed, "To American tourists," even though she technically wasn't a tourist.

"I would ask how your holiday is going . . ." Haley left the sentence hanging.

"Gall dang it! That woman has been the bane of my existence ever since Bérénice and I were married."

"You make it sound like Madame Chapdelaine died just to spite you."

"I wouldn't put it past her, except she would've done anything but die and go to hell just to torment me."

Haley blinked back her surprise at the man's outburst. "I'm surprised you came to visit her at all.

Madame Miller and Madame Chapdelaine didn't behave like long-separated sisters at the garden party. I didn't realise until later that they were related."

Mr. Miller shrugged. "The sisters were very different."

Haley had to agree. They hadn't even looked alike. One must've taken after the father while the other took after the mother.

Haley changed tack. "How's business?"

"Excuse me?"

"I understand you're a businessman," Haley said, then with a smile added, "just making conversation."

"Business is fine," he replied tersely. Then, after a sip of whisky, asked, "What about you? What are you doing at a Parisian bar in the middle of the day?"

"Your sister-in-law was poisoned, and the glass she drank from came from this bar," Haley answered bluntly.

"Is that so?"

"Have you come to the bar before, Mr. Miller? Say, any time before Mrs. Reed's garden party?"

Mr. Miller slammed his glass, conspicuously empty, next to Haley's untouched sherry. He narrowed his now-glassy eyes. "Just what are you implying, Miss Higgins?"

"Is it true that you made a poor business move and needed your sister-in-law to bail you out?"

Mr. Miller's face turned tomato red. He leaned over the table and sneered. "You'd best let the police do their jobs and keep your nose out of my affairs."

"Is that a threat, Mr. Miller?"

"It's fair warning." Mr. Miller placed his hat on his head, then left the bar without another word.

Haley wondered if she'd just kicked a bees' nest. She paid the barmaid for Mr. Miller's drink since he had left in a huff without paying, thanking the woman before leaving herself.

Seeing that she had a bit of time on her hands before her next stint at the hospital, Haley decided to head back to the villa. The fact that Beaufort and the two maids being present at both the garden party and the fashion parade was a coincidence that couldn't be overlooked.

After arriving at the villa, Haley paid the taxicab driver to wait for her until she returned. A summer storm had stirred up over the morning and cast an ominous shadow over the white stone villa, and Haley paused as the sky flashed with sheet lightning. Shaking off the eerie shivers that ran down her spine, she strode to the front door and rang the bell, a melodious running of notes.

Soon it was opened by Beaufort himself. His expression flickered with emotion—a mix of impatience and disdain?—before smoothing out dispassionately. "Mademoiselle Higgins," he said.

"Hello," Haley said lightly. "As you know, Mrs. Reed is in the hospital, and she asked me if I'd come by to pick up some of her things."

"Of course," Beaufort said, ushering her inside. "Allow me to summon Elise to accompany you upstairs."

Haley knew very well where Ginger's room was located, but it was obvious now that her status at the villa had been reduced from guest to visitor. Beaufort rang a bell, and then waited with Haley silently, his white-gloved hands tucked behind his back, as if Haley was suspected of having sticky fingers and merited watching.

She was pleased with the opportunity to converse with the footman. "Beaufort, I hope you don't mind me bringing up a matter of unpleasantness. You are aware of my cooperation with the hospital and the police in the matter of Madame Chapdelaine's death. Can you tell me, have you had any previous encounters with the fashion designer? Maybe at another gala or similar occasion?"

Beaufort lifted his chin. "Yes, mademoiselle. I've had the distinct pleasure."

Haley thought she caught a note of sarcasm in his voice. She asked, "Have you ever had an unpleasant experience?"

"I don't know what you're trying to suggest, mademoiselle."

"Only if you might be able to comment on Madame Chapdelaine's reputation. It might help shed light on why someone would wish her harm."

"I couldn't speak out of turn, mademoiselle."

"Yes, I know. I understand the class system is prevalent in Europe, but I'm American. We're all equal under God." She softened her eyes. "You can be honest with me."

"Off the record, mademoiselle?"

Haley wasn't a reporter, but she nodded. "Off the record."

"Madame Chapdelaine was, shall I say, very indiscriminate when it came to her intimate partners."

It had been clear to Haley, and surely everyone at the garden party, that the fashion designer was licentious. But did her objects include servants?

"Would you count yourself amongst her conquests?" Haley asked daringly.

A crimson blush ran up Beaufort's neck, a non-verbal sign of admission, but unfortunately, Elise chose that impromptu moment to join them.

The maid bobbed. "Mademoiselle Higgins."

"Please show Mademoiselle Higgins to Madame Reed's chamber," Beaufort said stiffly. "She needs a few moments to collect some of Madame Reed's things."

His message to Haley was loud and clear: get what you came for and leave.

16

Ginger managed to eat a small breakfast consisting of a croissant with butter and a cup of coffee. She was sitting comfortably in her bed when Inspector Tremblay arrived. With his hat in hand, he proclaimed, "Madame Reed, I am happy to see that you are alive and well!"

"As am I," Ginger said. Though she was a little groggy and a little weak in the legs, she felt like one might after experiencing a touch of influenza.

Inspector Tremblay pointed to an empty chair. "Do you mind?"

"Not at all," Ginger said. "I was expecting you."

"You were?"

"Well, I've been targeted by a potential poisoner

three days after a woman died of poisoning in the villa where I'm staying."

"You are clever," Inspector Tremblay said.

Ginger didn't think her deductions were all that sophisticated, and not for the first time, wondered at the inspector's low opinion of the capacity of female intelligence.

Inspector Tremblay fidgeted with an unlit pipe. "Why do you think you and Madame Sabine Chapdelaine were both targeted?"

"I really couldn't say," Ginger answered honestly.

"How well did you know Madame Chapdelaine? Were you good friends?"

"We were friendly, of course," Ginger said, "but I knew her mostly by reputation."

"Through fashion? I understand you run your own dress shop in London."

"That's correct on both counts. The fashion parade was why I had decided to stay an extra week in Paris after my family left."

Now that was over, for her at least, Ginger supposed she could head back to London a couple of days early. Basil didn't know about her present overnight stay at the hospital, and perhaps she should send off another telegram. But she didn't want him to worry, and it was much easier to relay a perilous story after the fact, once the danger had been eradicated.

Yes, she should go home and leave this case to the authorities.

"Madame?"

"Oh, sorry, Inspector. My mind drifted. What was it you were saying?"

"Is it possible that you were not poisoned at all but simply had a bad sandwich, or perhaps—" Inspector Tremblay stroked his moustache. "—perhaps you are the type of lady who likes attention."

Ginger gaped. "Are you suggesting I endangered my health to put myself in the spotlight? Whatever for?"

Inspector Tremblay shrugged. "The gentler sex is often irrational and dramatic. They are the reason smelling salts are so popular."

A heat brewed in Ginger's chest. "You undermine my reputation with clichéd stereotypes based on gender and interest in fashion?"

Another shrug. "I don't mean to offend, madame—"

"And yet you do it anyway."

"It is a hazard that comes with my work," the inspector said. "There is another reason one might pretend to be a poison victim: diverting the police."

Ginger held in a scoff. "You think I killed Madame Chapdelaine?"

"You planned the garden party, *non?*" Inspector Tremblay narrowed his eyes. "You invited your fashionable friends so that you could include Madame Chapdelaine. You invited her to spend the night."

"I did no such thing."

"I have a witness who says otherwise."

Louis, likely. Blast him!

"It's a simple thing for you to poison Madame Chapdelaine's drink and push her into your pool, then run upstairs to the nursery to create an alibi."

"I see you've thought this through," Ginger said tersely. "And what would be my motive?"

"That is what I plan to uncover, madame." He tapped each end of the fingers of one hand with the index finger of the other. "Jealousy? Money? Greed? Betrayal?" He raised a brow. "Love?"

France was liberal in its views on sexuality, especially when compared with Britain, and lovers of the same gender were, if not accepted, tolerated.

Ginger lifted her chin in defiance. "It seems you

have your work cut out for you, Inspector Tremblay. Now, if you don't mind, I'm rather tired."

"*Très bien.*" The inspector rose to his feet, carrying his hat with him as he walked to the door. "We will stay in touch, eh, Madame Reed? I trust you will remain in Paris for the time being."

Ginger patted her bed. "I believe I'll be here for a while, Inspector."

The man nodded, leaving Ginger to stew. Even before the inspector's instruction to stay in Paris, Ginger had decided she wasn't going anywhere. She couldn't trust this man to solve the case, and like Haley, Ginger didn't plan on spending any time in a French prison.

THE FIRST THING Ginger did after Inspector Tremblay left was to peek out of the door into the corridor. A uniformed officer sat in a nearby chair, his eyes on all the activity on the floor. There was a reason she'd been placed in a private room. She'd been told it was for her protection, but after the inspector's accusations, she suspected it was to keep her from leaving.

Finding her clothes folded in the drawer of the

cabinet beside her bed, Ginger removed the hospital gown she wore and put them on. She hated the thought of donning anything but fresh clothing, but one must do what one must do.

She had to be quick, as she didn't feel strong enough to take on a sturdy nurse. She was still formulating a way to distract the guard when she heard a tap on the door. Ginger found she had good reflexes under the circumstances—jumping back into bed and tugging firmly on the sheets until they were under her chin.

She turned her face, expecting to greet a nosy nurse, when, to her astonishment, Louis, or should she say, Roger Bernard, appeared, limping into the room with his uneven gait.

Ginger sat up and narrowed her eyes at the man. "How did you get past the officer?"

"Hello to you, too, Ginger," Louis said with a grin.

Ginger craned her neck, trying to see past Louis. "You didn't injure the poor fellow, did you?"

"I'm pleased you think so highly of my presumed abilities," Louis said, "but the man is unharmed. I only had to reassure him that we were very old friends from the war years and I was coming to bring moral support." He patted his chest. "You'll note that my jacket has been confiscated, and I can assure you I've been thoroughly patted down." He pointed to the door, which remained cracked open. "Another negotiated term."

Louis had stepped aside, allowing Ginger a visual line of sight, and the shoulder of the officer could be seen. "I promise not to scream," she said.

Lowering himself into the chair, Louis snorted. "That would be very mean-spirited of you."

"So, why are you here?" Ginger couldn't help sounding impatient. Louis' untimely arrival was impeding her intentions of making a quick getaway.

"To offer moral support, as I said."

Ginger glared back. "You just missed Inspector Tremblay. He accused me of murder."

"Tremblay accuses everyone."

"Even you?"

Louis laughed. "Especially me, I think. I'm surprised I didn't spend the night in *la taule*."

Ginger frowned at the thought of Louis sitting in jail. "Are you here because you have information?"

"Ah, now there's my girl." Louis casually crossed his legs. "I have a nibble, but until I can get proof, I'd rather not hypothesise."

"We've circled back to why you're here," Ginger said.

"I'm sincerely concerned for your welfare. Despite us getting off on the wrong foot this time, we were allies. *Are* allies. I am on your side, Ginger."

"All right. Then perhaps you can do me a favour?"

"Let me guess. You want to get past the eagle-eyed police officer."

Ginger smirked. "You do know me."

"Well," Louis lifted his chin. "You are dressed for it."

The sheet had fallen, revealing the lack of her hospital gown. "Touché."

"There is something I'd like to ask you first," Louis said.

Ginger held out a palm. "Stop there. I didn't kill Sabine Chapdelaine and didn't poison myself as a decoy."

"It seems you know me as well, Antoinette LaFleur."

Ginger retorted, "Louis."

Louis placed a finger on a cleanly shaven chin. "But you didn't stay LaFleur, did you?"

Ginger blinked. So few people knew this. She had used the alias LaFleur for most of the war, but a regrettable turn of events had caused her cover to be blown. Captain Smithwick, her commander, had sent her back to England on sudden leave, and when she returned to France, she was given a new name. And a haircut. Ginger liked to tease herself and say she brought in the bobbed hairstyle that grew in popularity after the war. She considered it one of her many contributions to society.

She flipped the sheets off her legs. "I don't know what you're talking about." With her toes, she dug for her shoes which were tucked under the bed. "Besides, it hardly matters now."

Louis gave her a look but didn't argue. She buckled up her sandals, fished her handbag out of the top drawer, and put the strap over her head.

"What's your big plan?" Louis asked.

"Can you feign an injury? You know—" Ginger nodded to Louis' weak leg.

"I might be able to refocus the officer, but it would draw the nurses' attention."

Good point.

"I suppose you'd be against whacking him on the head with something."

"And go to jail for assaulting a police officer and aiding a fugitive?" Louis shook his head. "No."

"What about a distraction?" Ginger said.

"You want me to create a scene at the other end of the corridor?"

"Is there a stairwell at this end?"

"There is."

"Marvellous." Ginger clapped her hands in eager anticipation. "Let's do it before the nurse comes again."

Louis' eyes seemed to sparkle, and Ginger wondered if he missed operating covertly. There wasn't a lot of call for it now unless one worked privately as an investigator as she did.

"How will I find you?" Louis asked.

Ginger had already worked out her next steps. "Dr. Lyon will know."

She watched through the crack in the door as Louis collected his jacket from the policeman, wincing as he threaded his arms into the sleeves. He complained about his war injury, *"de la guerre"*, before thanking the officer and hobbling away.

It was difficult for one to take one's eyes off the man. He had a handsome face, striking dark eyes, and carried himself in a melancholy but debonair way. In another man, his limp might've induced pity, but with Louis—Roger Bernard—it produced intrigue. Even the men in the corridor, including the police officer guarding Ginger's room, seemed taken.

When Louis took a stumble—and Ginger would have to thank him later for subjecting himself to this mild indignity—she slipped out of her room, walking cautiously in the other direction until she found the steps, hurrying down them until she found her way out.

17

Ginger's taxicab motored up the villa's long drive. She fought impatience, willing the driver to put a little weight on the accelerator. He seemed far too tentative around other motorists and pedestrians. From Ginger's experience, people knew well enough how to jump out of the way of a moving machine. At least she wasn't back in the day of the hansom cab, though there were several horses still working in that capacity around the city.

When the driver finally stopped near the front door, Ginger paid him, then hurried inside with her handbag firmly in her grip.

The entrance hall was empty, and her heels echoed click-clacking noises as she raced upstairs to the nursery. She'd been away from Rosa for too long, and her mama's heart was aching with irrational anxiety.

"Madam?" Nanny Green said when she saw Ginger. Rosa was balanced on her hip. "You're back. Thank goodness. I've been a wreck with worry. If it weren't for Miss Higgins bringing reassuring news, I wouldn't have known what to do, holding up in a foreign country, as it were."

"Miss Higgins was here?" Ginger asked.

"Yes, madam." The nanny's eyes flickered with confusion. "She came for some of your things, for your stay at the hospital."

Ginger wondered why Haley would do that and regretted the shock her friend was certain to get when she arrived at the hospital to find that Ginger was no longer there.

Ginger reached for Rosa, and Nanny Green handed the child over. Ginger kissed her daughter's head, stroked the wisps of dark curls from her face, and gave her a good looking over.

"Mummy's back, Rosa. I missed you!"

Rosa grabbed for Ginger's cheek. Ginger held out her finger instead, and the toddler latched on to it with her little fist.

"Are we going back to London now, madam?" Nanny Green asked.

"Yes, well you are," Ginger said. "I would like you and Lizzie to take Rosa home."

Nanny Green's eyes widened in surprise. "Now?"

"There's no reason to dawdle," Ginger said. "I'll come as soon as I can."

"If you think it's best, madam."

"I do. I'll tell Lizzie to help you pack up Rosa's things. Only take what you can carry. I'll bring the rest with me. Time is of the essence. If you leave quickly, you can get to Calais in time to catch the last boat to Dover."

"What shall I say to the villa staff, madam?" Nanny Green asked. She was an intelligent woman, and Ginger knew she could see past Ginger's forced nonchalance.

"Perhaps we'll let them think you've gone sight-seeing for the afternoon," Ginger said. "It's not a lie, really. You'll see plenty of sights on the train to Calais. I don't mean to create subterfuge, but the fact remains that a lady was murdered on this property, and until the killer is caught, one can't be too careful."

"I understand, madam," Nanny Green said. "To

be truthful, I was feeling uneasy about remaining here anyway. We'll make a discreet exit. Will Mr. Reed know to expect us?"

"I'll be sure to send him a telegram informing him," Ginger said.

Ginger ran into Lizzie on the landing.

"Oh, madam, I was so worried! Are you all right?"

"I'm fine, Lizzie. Just a little fatigued. Will you help me to my room?" The pretence was in case other eyes or ears were present. Like all those in service, the villa staff was trained to be quiet and invisible. Ginger's years of investigative work had confirmed that those in service knew more about everyone's business than they let on.

Once she and Lizzie were safely in her bedroom, Ginger relayed the plans she'd made with Nanny Green. "I'm afraid I'll have to leave most of my things as they are for the time being, but if you'd be so good as to pack me an overnight bag before you prepare your own things, that would be appreciated. Then please assist Nanny Green."

"Overnight, madam?"

It wasn't the maid's concern how Ginger spent her time and with whom, but under the circumstances, Ginger knew Lizzie was asking out of concern, not nosiness. She reiterated her lack of trust in the staff.

"I intend to spend some time with Miss Higgins. Which reminds me, please pack up her belongings as well."

Haley was a light traveller and hadn't come to the villa with more than one bag. It would be a quick task for Lizzie.

Lizzie left, and Ginger quickly stepped out of her day-old clothing and slipped into a clean frock. She didn't have time to style her hair properly, so a brush and a hat would have to do. Checking her appearance in the mirror, Ginger felt satisfied. She didn't look like a lady who'd been assaulted with poison and had slept unwell in a hospital overnight.

She scribbled out a short message for Basil, telling him to expect Rosa and company home and that she was staying a few more days to spend time with Haley. Folding the note, she put it into her pocket to deliver to the telegraph office later, as there was no one in the villa she could trust to do it on her behalf.

When Ginger stepped back into the corridor, she was startled to see Elise walk by with a handful of towels. Had the maid been watching her movements in the house the whole time?

"Madame," she said with a bend to her knees. In French, she added, "I'm relieved to see you are well. Mademoiselle Higgins must've missed the good news."

"*Oui, moi aussi,*" Ginger said. "Miss Higgins wasn't mistaken, but the doctors changed their minds about me in the meantime. It's good to be back. I have no plans for the day but to relax."

"Would you like something to eat? Shall I request a meal be made up by Madame Dupris?"

"That would be lovely," Ginger said. "*Merci.*"

The maid bobbed again, then headed towards the servant stairwell that opened up in the kitchen area. Ginger took the staircase that curved down to the entrance hall. Taking a cautious look around, she slipped unnoticed into the sitting room where the old-style candlestick telephone was located. She dialled the operator, asked for a taxicab to be engaged, and then asked for the hospital mortuary.

Haley wasn't in to take her call, so Ginger left a message with Dr. Lyon. After returning the cone-shaped receiver to its stand, Ginger left the sitting room in time to see Cosette disappear into another room. It wasn't unusual to see maids bustling about, and perhaps Ginger was making too much of it. She mustn't forget there were other suspects.

The Rocheforts and the Millers couldn't be discounted.

Though Ginger had allowed Elise to have the cook prepare her lunch, she had no intention of eating or drinking anything from the kitchen. Having one's stomach pumped once in a lifetime was enough.

The taxicab arrived and Ginger found she couldn't quite breathe comfortably until she saw her maid, daughter, and nanny climb in and the vehicle pull out of the driveway.

When she went back inside, Elise was there to announce that her lunch was ready.

"Do give my regrets to Madame Dupris. I've decided to meet a friend for lunch instead. Please ask Beaufort to ring a taxicab."

Elise's expression briefly showed disappointment, but propriety prevailed. She curtsied before leaving. "Yes, madame."

Ginger went back upstairs to collect the overnight bag that Lizzie had packed for her, Haley's suitcase, and her satchel. She was halfway down the staircase, unable to deny her present weakness when Beaufort saw her.

"Madame! Please allow me!"

Ginger let the footman do his job. He also

glanced at her with a glimmer of suspicion, and she guessed it had to do with Haley's ruse. She quickly mollified him. "The doctors decided I was well enough to return to the villa after all." That seemed to satisfy the footman and he left with her suitcases. He was quick about it, and by the time she got outside, he had not only deposited the bags on the steps, but he had emptied the mailbox.

"Post for you, madame," he said as he handed over two envelopes.

Ginger smiled as she recognised Scout's scribbly handwriting. She'd read it later when she had more time.

The other had a Parisian postmark. Not wanting to open the letter with Beaufort watching, Ginger waited until the taxicab arrived and she was seated inside. She ripped the envelope open with a long fingernail, and her breath hitched as she read:

"*C'est vous qui devriez mourir.*" It's you that should have died.

aley first checked for Dr. Lyon in his office and, finding it empty, took the extra steps to the mortuary and knocked on the door. She was greeted with a faint "*Entrez*," and stepped inside.

"Oh, *bonjour*, Mademoiselle 'Iggins," he said. "I expected you earlier."

"*Bonjour*," Haley returned. "I had an errand to run after visiting Madame Reed upstairs."

"*Oui, oui*," Dr. Lyon said with a bob of his head. "How is she? Well, I hope."

"Quite well, under the circumstances. Have you confirmed the results of her tests?"

They had reserved the contents of Ginger's stomach after it had been pumped and run tests for every conceivable ailment and poison they could think of, though Haley only had a hand in a few tests. Samples were sent to the hospital laboratory, where most of the testing occurred.

"You were right," Dr. Lyon said.

Haley pushed out her lips at the news. "Cyanide?"

Dr. Lyon nodded soberly. "I am afraid so. You were wise to administer Solutions A and B. I believe that saved her life."

Haley slowly lowered herself into a chair, staring blindly at the drab room. "I can't think how it could've been administered. She and I were given drinks simultaneously, and I didn't smell anything unusual about them, certainly not burned almonds."

"I have not received a report regarding other persons becoming ill that evening," Dr. Lyon said. "It is strange, indeed."

Haley stood. "I must apologise for not keeping the schedule I was given for my practicum. I've reached out to my professors and the other doctors I'm occasionally assigned to."

"I hope they've been understanding?" Dr. Lyon said.

"Yes, for now."

"And I am as well." Dr. Lyon scratched his

temple. "That reminds me, Madame Reed called here earlier, looking for you."

Haley ducked her chin as she imagined Ginger harassing the nurses to let her use their instrument at the nurses' desk.

"Did she leave a message?" Haley asked.

"*Oui*. She told me to tell you that the gold package is at your flat." Dr. Lyon wrinkled his nose as his gaze moved to the side. "Or was it the golden package? I suppose they mean the same thing."

Haley frowned. "Would you excuse me, Dr. Lyon? I think it best that I go upstairs and check on Madame Reed myself."

"*Certainement*." Dr. Lyon smiled. "Give her my regards."

Haley slipped through the mortuary door, then jogged to the stairwell, skipping up the stairs as quickly as she could. This was when trousers would've come in handy, but it was bad enough that she got looks for being tall or taller than most men; wearing trousers only added to the spectacle. If she wanted half a chance of blending in, she had to conform to the style of the times. At least the trend of shapeless frocks allowed for less encumbered movement.

She was out of breath when she reached Ginger's room.

A nurse came up behind her and clicked her tongue with disapproval. "If you are looking for Madame Reed, she is gone. The police are outraged. Can you believe that silly inspector accused us of not doing our jobs properly? Was it not his officer that let the lady slip by? *Imbéciles!*" The nurse turned on her flat leather shoes and entered the ward next door.

Haley was torn. Should she get back on track with her practicum requirements or return to her flat where the "gold package", most certainly Ginger herself, was waiting? Haley let out a short breath, then hurried down the stairwell until she made it outside and hailed a taxicab. She had to be sure that Ginger was in good health and unharmed.

ONE NEVER KNEW when a set of lock picks would come in handy, and Ginger made a point to always carry hers with her. Haley was staying in a building next to the hospital with small rooms—that were called bedsits in London—specifically for students and nurses. Picking the old lock on Haley's studio door was shamefully easy.

The lone window inside shed a minimal amount

of natural light, the rays shining dust beams onto the wooden floor. There was a bed, a wardrobe with a matching chest of drawers, a desk, a sink, and a small cupboard with a gas ring. The loo was at the end of the corridor and shared by all the occupants on the floor.

Textbooks towered on the desk and were stacked on the bedside table. Ginger browsed the titles, all complicated medical tomes, and realised she'd never seen her friend read a novel just for pleasure.

Feeling parched, Ginger poured a glass of water for herself, triggering a pang of hunger. She unbuckled her T-strap shoes and tossed them to the side, then settled herself on Haley's bed. Being the forward-thinking sort, she'd stopped at a sandwich stand on her way and now removed the wrapped cheese sandwich from her handbag and took a bite. Crumbs exploded from the crusty bun—no one made nearly impenetrable crusts like the French.

"My apologies, Haley," Ginger mumbled as she brushed the crumbs off the quilt. The bed was just about wide enough for two, and it was quite likely she'd be sharing it with Haley that night. The thought of crumbs in the bed had her flipping her legs over the edge and strolling to the lone wooden chair.

Her gaze settled on the neighbouring brick wall, which was the sum of the view out of the window, and she laughed mirthlessly. To think that only four days earlier, at a grand villa, she had been hosting a garden party for esteemed members of the Parisian fashion industry, wearing a Jean Patou gown and drinking top-notch champagne.

And now she waited alone in a small flat intended for poor students, eating a street sandwich and drinking tap water. What would Basil think if he could see her now? The note inscribed for a telegram to him was still folded and in her pocket. A telegraph office was down the street, and she'd send the note off as soon as she and Haley had caught up.

Ginger checked her wristwatch. It'd been several hours since she'd left her message with Dr. Lyon. Had he given the message to Haley by now? Ginger frowned. What if he'd forgotten? Haley would most certainly return to the villa. But, on seeing her things removed and none of Ginger's family or Ginger herself, she'd naturally come back to her flat. Ginger only hoped Haley wouldn't give anything away to the staff there. No, she wouldn't. Haley was far too intelligent for that.

The doorknob rattled as someone on the other side of the door Ginger had locked attempted to gain entrance. Ginger stiffened as she called out, "Who is it?"

Haley's voice reached her, "It's me," and Ginger relaxed. Haley unlocked the door and stepped inside.

Haley smirked when she saw Ginger there. "I'm not even going to ask how you got in."

"Because you already know," Ginger said with a wry smile. Ginger had introduced Haley to her lock-picking skills for the first time when they'd worked on a case together on the SS *Rosa*.

Haley looked pointedly at Ginger's half-eaten sandwich. "You must be feeling better."

"I am. Hartigan ladies are made of sturdy material."

Haley laughed. "I've known three, and yes, you are right." She climbed onto her bed, shifting into the position Ginger had recently occupied. "Hey, are these crumbs?" She scowled at Ginger with indignation. "Were you eating that on my bed?"

"I confess, I hadn't thought it through," Ginger said, "but quickly vacated once the hazard became clear."

"So, where are the rest of the troops?" Haley asked.

"The ruse is they're out for a day of sightseeing

in the city. The truth is they're on a train back to Calais."

"Clever." Haley pulled out the pins that held up her faux bob, deposited them on her bedside table, and let her dark curls fall loose. "Am I to assume you're staying with me tonight?"

"If you don't mind."

"Well, I suppose it's only fair that I return the favour, having imposed on you plenty of times, so long as you're okay with it being a little tight."

"It's cosy!" Ginger said with childlike glee. "We can think of it as a pyjama party."

"You brought pyjamas?" Haley asked.

Ginger pointed to her handbag. "I left the villa on the pretence I was returning, but I did pack night things."

Haley let out a breath. "You're nothing if not resourceful."

"Though I understand you were there to collect some of my things as well?" Ginger raised a red brow. "I hope that does include my hairpins, as I couldn't find them anywhere."

Haley reached into her handbag and dropped the box of pins onto the chest of drawers, along with a number of headscarves. "Elise waited for me in the hallway, so I had to make a show of getting something, and I'd left the taxi driver in the driveway for long enough."

"What was it that you hoped to accomplish there?" Ginger asked.

"I wanted to talk to Beaufort," Haley replied. "I find it a little too convenient that he was at both the garden party and the fashion parade, and in your case, very close to the scene."

"Did he reveal anything?"

"Without saying so directly, he suggested that Madame Chapdelaine liked to have trysts with the male staff, particularly those of a younger persuasion."

"Interesting," Ginger said. "Perhaps Beaufort had had his heart broken."

"And sought his revenge," Haley added. "And then went after you because he feared you were getting too close to discovering the truth."

Ginger looked at her friend with concern. "That would put you in similar danger now, would it not?"

"I suppose it would."

"I also have news," Ginger said.

"Good news?" Haley asked hopefully.

"No, I'm afraid it's rather grim." Ginger reached for her handbag and removed the note. "It appears that I was the intended victim all along."

Haley frowned as she read the short script. "Any idea where it came from?"

"None." Ginger held out the untouched half of her sandwich. "Have you eaten?"

Haley eyed the offering. "You don't want it?"

Ginger placed a palm on her stomach. "I don't want to overdo it."

"Good idea." Haley accepted the sandwich. After a bite, she asked, "Won't the villa staff be concerned if you don't return?"

"They retire early. I told Beaufort not to wait up."

"But you think one of them will?"

Ginger stifled a yawn. "Possibly. If Beaufort or one of the others is the killer."

Haley finished the sandwich and wiped her mouth with her fingertips. "You look exhausted, Ginger, and it's not surprising after what you've been through. I suggest we start this pyjama party sooner rather than later."

Ginger wanted to protest, but sudden heavy fatigue made her nod. "Shall I prepare myself first?" she asked. She didn't relish using a public toilet, but one did as one must.

"After you," Haley said.

Ginger ventured down the long corridor, keeping

her shoes on. Low murmurings from a wireless filtered through the walls and competed with the whistle of a kettle on a gas ring.

The bathroom sink's lighting did little to assuage her fears about looking sickly and frail, but it was nothing a good night's sleep couldn't fix.

She chuckled at her tired image in the mirror. It would be miraculous to sleep well in that little bed, especially when sharing it. As they said, beggars couldn't be choosers, and it wasn't like she hadn't slept in more uncomfortable conditions during the war.

When Ginger returned to the room, Haley was ready to take her turn and left her friend alone to put on her pyjamas—camisole and pantaloons made of pink silk and trimmed with wide lace. They didn't exactly fit the situation, but they would suffice. Ginger slipped into Haley's bed, keeping herself close to one edge, and instantly fell into a deep sleep. She was unaware of Haley's presence until the morning light shone through the windows and awakened her.

19

The next morning, Haley ventured out and brought breakfast back to the flat—fresh, buttery croissants with jam, and strong, creamy coffee, both of which delighted Ginger greatly. "You're a saint," she said, accepting her portion.

Haley pulled out the newspaper she had tucked under one arm. "You'll be very interested in seeing today's headlines. Le Suspect de Meurtre Arrêté."

"In the Chapdelaine case?" Ginger snatched the paper from Haley's outstretched hands. "Who?" Her eyes fell on the suspect's name as Haley answered her question.

"Brian Miller."

"Oh mercy." Ginger read the article eagerly,

translating for Haley's sake. Brian Miller's financial woes were highlighted, and it was believed that he'd hoped for a loan or a financial gift from his sister-in-law. "It's presumed that the victim had refused and is alleged that Brian Miller killed her out of revenge," Ginger said, "perhaps thinking his wife would inherit."

"Would she?" Haley asked.

"Unless Madame Chapdelaine left a will stating otherwise," Ginger said, "and since she didn't have a spouse or children, then I imagine it would go to her sister."

"I suspect Mrs Miller would be held responsible for her husband's business debts," Haley said. "Unless she divorces. Maybe even then. I don't understand enough about family law to say."

"I don't either," Ginger said, "and with two nations involved, it could get tricky."

Haley inclined her head as she swatted curls off her face. "You must feel relieved."

Ginger let out a long breath. "I suppose I should, but . . ."

"But you don't think Brian Miller is guilty."

"The article doesn't state that definitive proof has been found," Ginger said. "It's circumstantial at best."

"Inspector Tremblay seemed eager to solve the case."

Ginger snorted. "Sabine Chapdelaine was a Parisian celebrity, and her loss was an impact on an important industry in France. I wonder how the inspector is explaining the attempt on my life. Surely he must see the connection between what happened to Madame Chapdelaine and me."

Haley smirked. "I don't think he cares as much about you, and you clearly aren't dead. He might even believe you've left France and are no longer his concern. But the connection is as plain as day. You and Sabine Chapdelaine had a lot in common. You resemble each other in looks, are both passionate about fashion, and you were poisoned at an event she was supposed to headline."

Ginger's mind returned to the fashion parade events leading to her collapse. "The perpetrator has to be someone who was at both my garden party and the fashion parade that evening."

"Agreed," Haley said. "And they are . . ."

"Gaspard Rochefort, Bérénice Rochefort, Lou—" She'd almost said Louis, but quickly corrected, "Roger Bernard, Brian Miller, Aurélie Miller, and the staff at the villa, Bruno Beaufort, Elise Cadieux and Cosette Padou."

"Eight is quite a lot of possibilities," Haley mused. "Though the Millers weren't at the fashion parade, which is another reason I'd rule them out and believe that Tremblay has the wrong man."

Ginger's thoughts were caught on one of the potential suspects. Haley noticed her blank look and asked, "Ginger? What is it?"

"Padou," Ginger said. "The surname is familiar to me."

"It's not all that uncommon," Haley said, "at least in these parts."

"I know, but—"

"But?"

Ginger shrugged. "I don't know. It'll come to me in time."

"Where do you want to start?" Haley asked.

"Why don't you mull it over," Ginger said, getting to her feet. "I feel terrible that I haven't sent Basil a telegram yet. I'll just run to the telegraph office down the street, and when I return, we'll make a plan."

"Very well." Haley reached for a textbook on the bedside table. "I have some reading to catch up on since these unfortunate events have caused me to miss some of my classes." As Ginger reached for the doorknob, she added, "Be careful out there."

Ginger took her time as she headed down the stairs, her mind not on Basil but on the name Padou. She hadn't been entirely truthful when telling Haley that her memory would come to her in time.

It had already come to her. And she needed to find Louis right away.

Louis—was his last name really Bernard?—had given her his card, but it lacked a telephone number. His address was listed, but it was too far from Haley's flat for Ginger to walk. She could hail a taxi-cab, but the journey would take too long, and Haley would become suspicious. Ginger didn't like with-holding information from her trusted friend, but she'd made an oath to the British King, and if it was in her power, she was determined to keep it.

The café where she and Louis had met for lunch wasn't too far away. People were creatures of habit. Was it possible he'd returned for lunch? The French ate later in the day than most British. It was worth a try.

When she reached the café, she searched the patio, which was half empty, and the inside seating areas as well. She was disappointed, though not surprised, when Louis wasn't to be found anywhere.

He probably ate his luncheon later, like many French did. Ginger decided to do a bit of window-shopping—a good excuse to explain her tardiness to Haley—and returned in an hour, only to be disappointed once more. She had given up and was about to head back to Haley's flat when a taxicab pulled to a stop, and Louis stepped out.

He smiled when he saw Ginger standing there.

"Madame Reed." He tipped his hat. "What a pleasant surprise."

"Will you walk with me, Monsieur Bernard?" Ginger asked. "I'm on my way to the telegraph office. My husband is waiting for a telegram from me."

"Keeping track of the wife, is he?" Louis returned with a grin.

Miffed at the man's arrogance, she returned, "The rest of my family has returned to England, and I must inform him of the new situation."

"How will he feel about you staying behind?" Louis said. "Particularly after your brush with death." He grinned again. "You look fabulous, by the way."

Ginger picked up her pace, not wanting or needing to respond to Louis' pertinent questioning. However, she was soon reminded of Louis' limp, and compassion prompted her to slow her gait.

"Might I presume your interest in the death of Madame Chapdelaine remains as strong as before?" Louis asked.

"You might." Ginger slowed her stride slightly, keeping her eyes on the movement of the pedestrians and side-stepping when necessary. "I hoped we could speak frankly, having worked together before."

"My recollections of the war are crystal clear, madame." Louis' gaze grew serious, and for once, he didn't look at her as if he was about to make an improper proposition.

"The name Padou," she said. "Does it ring a bell?"

"Aha, madame, I am ahead of you. As a long-time resident of Paris, I have access to information that would be difficult for you to access, especially with limited time. I became very interested in all the potential suspects, especially once my neck was on the line."

Ginger locked her eyes on Louis. "What did you learn?"

"Everyone has secrets, madame, but some aren't really secrets. Just forgotten tragedies."

"Are you speaking of Monsieur Padou?" Ginger had met many people during the war, but M. Padou had stood out in how he violently approached his work as a chef.

"*Oui, madame,*" Louis said.

Ginger's mind immediately went back to the end of 1917. The trauma of that evening hit her like a dark wave.

20

Her mission that evening in Rethel was to pose as a waitress at a New Year's Eve party hosted by Generaloberst Albrecht Balsinger. He was a handsome man with striking blue eyes and close-cropped blond hair and was one of Germany's most prominent war leaders. Because of the Generaloberst's prominence, the security around the small château would be unusually tight. Ginger's superiors decided that she would present herself as a working girl from a nearby town, rather than appear in her usual guise as Mlle Antoinette LaFleur, because of her skills in speaking French and German. Antoinette would never serve drinks at a party and, even if invited to such an affair, wouldn't be ignored like a humble serving girl who could unobtrusively eavesdrop. For that night, she was Mlle Clarisse Baton from the town of Amagne.

The size of the party meant additional staff would be needed, and because of specific covert contacts within the staff of the château, the hiring of Clarisse Baton was certain. Ginger had been paired with another operative, a Frenchman she knew as Louis, who joined her as a waiter. She and Louis worked on opposite sides of the room and only conversed when the job required it.

The party's extravagance had been striking, especially during wartime when many French people were close to starving. The Germans had seized most wheat and potato crops, eggs, and cattle. To see huge plates of roast beef, potatoes, devilled eggs, fresh vegetables, and ham being presented on long tables adorned with bottles of fine French wine and champagne had been dizzying. The hors d'oeuvres alone would have fed many households of impoverished French in the town.

Ginger and Louis' task was to listen in on conversations by anyone high up in the military, of which there were quite a few at that New Year's Eve celebration. A rumour of a huge German offensive planned for early spring had their superiors on edge. As the evening wore on, large amounts of brandy were consumed, and the officers' tongues loosened. Ginger picked up snatches of conversation about that very subject.

Chef Jean Padou, a thirty-year-old man, was considered a prodigy in the kitchen. He had made a name for himself because of his culinary talent, not his temperament. His demeanour was abrupt, and his mouth sharper than the knives he wielded so expertly. None dared to cross him, fearing job loss or, at the very least, a severe tongue-lashing.

Ginger couldn't afford to be fired or openly degraded, so she gave the man a wide berth. She'd been told he worked with his sister, the only one who could calm him when his rage exploded. They had a similar look, dark hair and high cheekbones, and Ginger kept her distance from them.

Things were going relatively well until Generaloberst Balsinger caught Ginger's eye. Though she'd quickly looked away, he did not divert his gaze. She'd kept her head down and her hands busy cleaning away dirty ashtrays and empty glasses; even so, she could sense the Generaloberst staring at her. Sweat droplets formed on her upper lip, and as she casually brought her hand to her face, she risked a look in the Generaloberst's direction. Her mission and her safety depended on her being unassuming.

She'd let her shoulders relax when she saw that his attention had been captured elsewhere, but her relief was short-lived. The object of his distraction was his wife, an Austrian lady with the Christian name of Gertrude, who seemed none too pleased. Her husband's tendency to wander was well known, much to the lady's mortification, and after a few sharp words which Ginger couldn't hear, Frau Balsinger's eyes, flashing with anger, landed on Ginger.

Before she could turn away and make her escape from the room, the hostess stormed over. "What is your name, mademoiselle?"

Without making eye contact, Ginger returned in French, "I am Clarisse Baton, madame."

"You are a pretty girl, Clarisse. Your red hair is unusual, though appealing." Her use of Ginger's first name struck Ginger as very direct—as if Ginger were her servant.

"I . . . thank you, madame."

Frau Balsinger cocked her head, looking at Ginger as if she were a strange insect pinned onto a corkboard for examination. "But I imagine you to be flighty like most young French women are." Her mouth formed into a cruel, hard line, and her eyes showed contempt.

"I, um guests need more to drink," Ginger said, "and my tray is empty." In search of a way to escape this public scrutiny, Ginger glanced at the kitchen area far on the other side of the hall.

Undaunted, Frau Balsinger said stiffly, "My husband has, er, an inclination for younger women." She lowered her voice and, with added menace, continued, "But you probably already knew that, Clarisse."

Over the lady's shoulder, Ginger could see Generaloberst Balsinger chatting with several other officers. Ginger started to walk away, but Frau Balsinger took a step to block her, grabbing her arm.

"Don't you dare walk away from me, Fräulein," she said with barely controlled anger. "I must leave for Berlin tomorrow morning, but I will be back in less than a week. My husband likes to have ridiculous dalliances from time to time, and I make allowances, but not with trollops like you. People in the house, in this town, work for me, do you understand? If you even so much as look at my husband while I'm gone, I will know."

She dramatically pivoted on her heels and glided away, but just when Ginger thought she'd escaped the snare, a familiar face entered the room through the main doors. Ginger's heart stopped cold.

The man was Hauptmann Gottlieb Auerswald, the brother of Frau Balsinger. He looked virtually the same as when Ginger had met him two years previously in northern France at a similar party. His uniform was still crisp and pressed, although he was still overweight, a testament to his carnal indulgences. At that party, Ginger had posed as his German date. He might recognise her if he spotted her, and her cover would be blown.

Because of Gottlieb Auerswald, Captain Smithwick had been reluctant to assign Ginger to her current mission. Still, Ginger had argued that the man was a lower-ranking officer and, despite his relationship with Frau Balsinger, wouldn't be invited to a party full of high-ranking officials. Besides, it had been believed that Hauptmann Auerswald had returned to Germany.

Ginger had been wrong.

Hauptmann Gottlieb Auerswald's laugh was boisterous as he greeted his fellow officers. As he made his way to his sister and Generaloberst Balsinger, Ginger wouldn't be able to make it past him to the kitchen or the rear of the building without directly crossing his path. She quickly moved towards a doorway that opened to a corridor that led to a storage area where she could hide.

Her absence would be noticed soon in the kitchen, and no one wanted to cross Chef Padou, especially at such an important event, so Ginger knew she couldn't wait long. Poking her head out of the door, she scanned the room, searching for Hauptmann Auerswald. When she didn't spot him anywhere, she walked as nonchalantly as she could through the crowd of people towards the kitchen and the rear exit near it.

Before she got halfway there, Hauptmann Auerswald appeared, seemingly out of nowhere. Ginger swiftly changed directions, but not before he saw her, their eyes locking. His expression went from jovial to puzzlement.

Blast it!

Instinctively, Ginger took the only route left to her, up the grand stairway that led to the next floor of the château. She tried not to look like she was in a hurry as she started up the stairs.

"Mademoiselle?"

Hauptmann Auerswald came from behind Ginger through the chatter of all the voices in the room. She didn't look back but sensed he was making his way through the guests to follow her.

She quickened her pace. When she reached the landing, she risked a quick look back. Hauptmann

Auerswald had now started up the stairway. Louis stood at the bottom of the stairs, his brown eyes as wide as saucers. Ginger subtly shook her head. *Do not follow. Do not get involved.*

Ginger's heart beat in near panic as she raced down the corridor. Once she saw it ended with no way out, she ducked into one of the huge bedrooms and closed the door. Finding a sturdy chair in front of an ornately decorated dressing table by the arched window, Ginger leaned it back and wedged it under the door handle. There was a good chance Hauptmann Auerswald had seen her enter the room, but hopefully, when he tried to open the door, he would think it locked and give up. If not, the chair would only hold briefly.

Looking wildly around the room, which was lavishly decorated and quite large, Ginger realised this was the bedroom that belonged to Generaloberst Balsinger and his wife.

The voice of Hauptmann Auerswald followed a knock on the door. "Fräulein? Don't be frightened. I only want to speak with you for a moment."

Ginger held her breath, and after a moment, the man's footsteps grew quieter as he went further along the corridor. He knocked on another door and called out again. It was clear he didn't know which room

Ginger had slipped into. There were three or four more rooms on this floor, all with closed doors but probably not locked. He would undoubtedly go into each one to search for her. It was only a matter of scant moments before he returned to this room.

A large, arched window had been left partially open to the cool night air. In near desperation, Ginger went to it and looked out. A metal trellis covered with seasonally dormant vines ran to the right. She put her hand on the trellis and pulled. It seemed sturdy enough and free of rust. The garden below was relatively snow-free, so she could escape without leaving tracks. Just a few metres away was an opening in a large hedge, and beyond that were several unlit avenues and alleyways. A fall would undoubtedly be injurious, and any wound to her ankle or leg would slow her, and soon afterwards, she'd be caught.

The clock tower, visible from this window, showed twenty-five minutes before midnight. For her own sake and that of Daniel, who had no idea of the peril for which she had volunteered, she had to do everything she could to stay free and alive as the calendar turned to 1918.

She had no choice but to climb out. Her dress would severely impede her progress, so she quickly removed her apron, skirt, and blouse, leaving her in her undergarments, then stuffed them under the bed, unkindly hoping that Frau Balsinger would be the first to find them there. Opening the massive wooden wardrobe, Ginger selected a woman's overcoat.

"*Danke*, Frau Balsinger." Ginger rushed to the window and dropped the coat, letting it fall to the ground below.

She had one leg out of the window when the doorknob turned.

The trellis turned out to be worthy, and though Ginger received several rude scratches on her arm, a bad cut on her hand, and a bruise on her shin, she made it to the ground. Grabbing the coat, she raced across the short garden, just barely keeping from slipping and falling on the frozen grass, and ducked behind the hedge. The light from the bedroom window suddenly darkened, and she knew without looking that Hauptmann Auerswald's portly frame was leaning out as he peered into the night.

As she ran along the length of the hedge and down a narrow alleyway, Ginger prayed he couldn't see her from his vantage point. She carefully made her way through a side street behind a bakery near her flat as she heard a distant church bell ring in the new year.

Later, Ginger got word about the consequences of her escape from Hauptmann Auerswald and Generaloberst Balsinger. Captain Smithwick had swiftly sent her back to England, where she changed her looks and was given a new identity.

Unfortunately, Generaloberst Balsinger hadn't taken kindly to the news that an English spy had been operating under his nose. As a result, he'd been disciplined and humiliated and had, in turn, disciplined and humiliated his kitchen staff. M. Padou hadn't survived the Generaloberst's violent outburst.

GINGER SHOOK her head to break the memory.

"Is everything all right, Madame Reed," Louis asked.

"Yes, of course," Ginger said. With a tilt of her head, she cautiously asked, "Is Cosette Padou a relation of Chef Padou's?"

Louis nodded soberly. "*Oui*. A sister."

21

Haley found it challenging to concentrate on her book: *Domestic Medical Practice.* She repeatedly glanced at her watch and then at the door. Why had she let Ginger go out alone? Her mind turned to the poisoning at the fashion parade, and despite the seriousness of the event, Haley comforted herself. The killer had a modus operandi. Ginger would hardly succumb to poisoning on her short trek to the telegraph office.

Another glance at her watch and Haley moaned. Ginger really should be back by now. However, Ginger was on her guard and capable of taking care of herself, something she had demonstrated time and time again.

Slapping the textbook shut, Haley stood, shoved

her fists into her pockets, and resisted pacing the small floor. What had they been talking about before Ginger left? Something had propelled her sudden departure.

Haley wasn't convinced Ginger had suddenly recalled a telegram to Basil was due . . . *Padou!* They'd discussed the list of suspects, and Ginger had pinpointed Cosette Padou. *Why?* And more to the point, why hadn't she discussed her thoughts about the maid with Haley?

Haley pulled her notebook out of her handbag and flipped the pages until she reached her notes about Cosette Padou. Ginger had gotten the staff addresses from Mme Dupris under the premise of sending a thank-you gift—which she had done—and had shared the information with Haley.

Haley had noted Cosette Padou's address and was surprised when she realised it was in a nicer area of Paris and not the kind of apartment a maid could afford to rent.

With another flick of the wrist to check the time, Haley decided to go to the telegraph office and hopefully find Ginger there. However, when she arrived five minutes later, she was disappointed to find that Ginger wasn't there.

Haley asked the clerk in stilted French, "Have you seen an English lady, pretty, with red hair?"

The clerk shook his head and replied, "No, mademoiselle."

Dang it! What was Ginger up to?

Outside, Haley scoured the sidewalks, and even on her tiptoes, which made her rather tall, she didn't spot Ginger's familiar form. Clearly, Ginger hadn't wanted her to know what she was doing, and Haley had to trust that Ginger had good reason.

Haley wasn't about to wait around and do nothing. She waved down a taxicab and gave the driver Cosette Padou's address. Like many apartment buildings in Europe, this one was built close to the street, several storeys high, and was made of limestone.

After knocking on the door, Haley was greeted by a young woman who was not Cosette. She was dressed in a jacket and hat as if she was about to leave.

"Oh, hello," Haley started, then continued in her stumbling version of French. "I am looking for Cosette."

The girl eyed Haley warily. "You don't look like a friend of hers."

"We met briefly. I have a couple of questions. Is she in?"

The girl shook her head. "I am Giselle, Cosette's lodger." She stared at Haley with a bored expression. "I do not know how long she will be away. Who knows how long she will be or what she is doing? She can be strange sometimes."

"Strange how?" Haley asked.

Giselle shrugged. "She broods. Stares into space. Plays with her chemistry equipment. Strange like that."

Haley's breath caught when Giselle mentioned the chemistry equipment. Maybe Cosette was an odd bird, but a young woman with a chemistry equipment was indeed strange. Haley knew this from experience.

"We are not friends," Giselle continued. "She's giving me a good deal on rent; otherwise, I'd find someone else to live with."

Haley arched a brow. "You're renting from *her*?"

"This is her family home. She's the only one left now; sadly, her parents and brother are dead." Giselle smirked. "It's probably why she's so odd. You can wait for her if you like. I am just leaving."

"If you don't mind," Haley said. Her heart skipped with excitement at the opportunity to snoop around. "But you don't have to leave on my account."

Giselle wrinkled her nose. "I do not like this flat. Something is rotting in it. I always feel sick."

Haley sniffed but didn't smell anything rotting. Just the old smells of cooking oil and musk.

Satisfied that Haley didn't look like the thieving type, Giselle put on her gloves and left Haley alone.

The flat was decorated with simple pieces of furniture constructed in the previous century. One large framed painting hung over a chesterfield, depicting a family of four: mother, father, son, and daughter. Haley assumed the young girl in the painting was Cosette.

Haley held a quick breath when she entered a bedroom, which had to belong to Cosette due to the impressive chemistry equipment sitting on a table. The microscope was older, but a quick look proved to Haley it was still in working order. A tray of test tubes, vials of several shapes and sizes, and a collection of measuring utensils surrounded it. A shelf above the table held common household liquids like bleach, rubbing alcohol, and acetate. She also noted a container of laudanum and a small bottle of opium tincture. A nearby bookshelf contained volumes of chemistry-related textbooks on one shelf and, on another, a bunch of sealed jars, all assigned hand-written labels. Haley squatted low to read them. A small jar, half full, was marked *Chloroform*. Another was labelled *Arsenic* and another *Cyanide*.

Could Cosette Padou be their killer? But what was her motive? Had Ginger discovered it? Was that why she'd left? To confirm her theory?

Haley let out a breath as she straightened back up. The big question was why Ginger had not included her in her hypothesis. She was usually very open and talkative, especially when working on a puzzling case.

Except when she wasn't.

Haley had to concede that Ginger had some-times become uncharacteristically tight-lipped in the past. And every time Haley had time to examine everything and everyone concerned thoroughly, it came down to something that had happened during the war.

Ginger would never talk about that.

The front door slammed, and Haley was startled, grabbing her heart. Her instinct was to remove herself from Cosette's room before getting caught, but she was too late. Cosette Padou stood in the doorway to the bedroom, her crooked face blos-soming crimson as her eyes narrowed in a glare.

"Mademoiselle Higgins, imagine my surprise," she said stiffly, in English.

Haley held up her palms. "I do apologise. Giselle let me in."

"Why?"

"I was looking for you."

"Again, why?"

"Can we sit in the kitchen? We can chat, maybe over a cup of coffee?"

"You aren't my guest. I'm not making coffee."

"Very well." Haley made a move to slip past Cosette, but the maid blocked her way.

"You might tell me why you're snooping in my room."

"Yes, well, I became restless waiting and wandered a bit, and of course, when I saw your chemistry set-up, well, as a fellow scientist, I couldn't help but explore. And admire!" Haley added quickly.

Cosette's shoulders softened, her complexion returning to its normal pale state.

"I suppose I could make coffee," she said, smiling at last. "We can talk science."

Haley nervously followed the maid to the kitchen, believing that asking for a cup of coffee from a known poisoner hadn't been the smartest idea.

. . .

REGRETFULLY, Ginger had to leave Basil to hang a bit longer. She abruptly said her goodbyes to Louis, whose slower gait was a convenience to Ginger at this moment, and she scampered across the busy roadway, escaping him.

Not that she felt endangered by her old colleague in any way, but because she wanted to get back to Haley, who was likely checking her watch and pacing the floors in worry. And she wanted to tell Haley what she'd learned, if not exactly how she had learned it. Cosette Padou was dangerous and needed to be apprehended quickly. The question was how? Should they contact Inspector Tremblay? Would the man scoff and brush them off because of the flimsiness of their evidence? Sadly, Ginger didn't have tangible evidence in hand.

It was a problem that she and Haley would work out together.

Ginger was nearly out of breath by the time she reached the front entrance of Haley's apartment building and needed to take a moment to rest before taking on the stairs. Once refreshed, she headed to Haley's flat.

"Haley!" she said as she opened the door, this

time with the spare key Haley had given her. "Oh." The word slipped out as the situation was obvious. In a room as small as this one, there was no place for a person to hide. She was gone unless she was using the loo at the end of the corridor.

Ginger peeked down the corridor, and the bathroom door was closed. She'd wait a few minutes to see if Haley materialised. She was tempted to lie on the empty bed as she didn't have as much energy as usual after her recent poisoning. But since she couldn't risk falling asleep, she took the empty chair instead.

Everything was as it was when Ginger had left. The bed was neatly made, the window coverings drawn, clothes were hidden in the wardrobe, and shoes were under the bed. Her eyes landed on a notebook lying open on the desk. Usually, Ginger wouldn't peek into another person's private matters, but a name scribbled in large letters was hard to miss: Cosette.

Had Haley come to the same conclusion as Ginger from another perspective? Snatching the notepad, Ginger read the notations, which included Cosette's address.

Jumping to her feet, Ginger grabbed her handbag and locked the door behind her. The bathroom door was propped open and the room no longer occupied, but Ginger hadn't expected to see Haley there anyway. Haley had tired of waiting for Ginger and had gone to investigate on her own.

Ginger only hoped that she wouldn't arrive too late.

22

Cosette scooped coffee grounds into the percolator basket, and Haley claimed one of the two chairs at the table. Unfortunately, the table was situated away from the door, the kitchen in between them. Still, not so far that Haley couldn't make a run for it if things got dire.

At least, from this vantage point, she could watch Cosette's movements with hawk-like intensity. Cosette turned on the gas ring and placed the percolator on it. When the coffee finished brewing, she poured it into two coffee cups.

"You needn't watch me so severely," Cosette said as she brought over the coffee cups and the sugar. "I'm not going to poison you."

Haley feigned a chuckle. "Why would I ever imagine that?"

Cosette sat across from Haley and said, "Because you think I killed Sabine Chapdelaine and tried to kill your haughty English friend."

Cosette blew on the surface of her coffee, then took a sip. "See, I'm drinking it too."

Haley would make sure Cosette took an honest swallow before she'd let any of it cross her own lips.

"Did you?" Haley asked.

Cosette grinned. "I'll not incriminate myself, mademoiselle. You should know by now; I'm cleverer than that."

"I have a high respect for your intelligence, Cosette."

Cosette nodded, then pushed the sugar bowl toward Haley. "Sugar?"

"Not today, thank you."

Cosette chuckled, then added a heaping teaspoon to her own cup. She sipped, and Haley watched her throat to ensure she took enough to swallow. "See? Not poisoned."

Haley touched her cup to her lips but didn't drink. There were poisons where a small amount ingested would do no harm, but a larger quantity might. Haley was determined to play it safe.

"What I don't understand," Haley said, "is what these two ladies, Madame Chapdelaine and Mrs. Reed, have to do with you?"

"That's because only one of them does. Mrs. Reed. The other was a mistake."

Haley's blood cooled. Ginger had been the intended victim all along? "I don't understand," she said.

Cosette took a longer sip, then nodded at Haley. "I'll explain after you drink your coffee. A sign of trust, if you will. You watched me prepare it. I'm a scientist, not a magician."

"How do I know my cup was empty to start with?" Haley said. "I would hope that you would respect my intelligence as well."

"Fine," Cosette said with a huff. "Deny yourself." She sipped again, then smiled crookedly. "Do you consider yourself a chemist, mademoiselle, or a biologist?"

"Biologist," Haley said, "though my work necessitates a working knowledge of chemistry."

"I've always been fascinated with chemistry," Cosette offered. "I would've gone to university if my brother hadn't died." Her gaze darkened.

Haley stared back with a look of question, saying nothing. Cosette filled in the silence.

"Jean was my elder by two years. Our mother died when we were little, and our father after the war. That was my father's chemistry equipment that you were admiring."

"You inherited your interest in science from him."

"And Jean inherited his love of cooking from my mother."

"Jean was a chef?"

"The best," Cosette said, her misshapen cheeks flushing with pride. "His excellence in the kitchen didn't go unnoticed by the Boche."

The mention of the German army caused Haley to shiver. The war had been a horrible experience for all, worse for some than others, and many never made it out alive.

"Jean and I were in Rethal when the Germans crossed the border. We were brought up by our grandmother after our mother died—father stayed here in Paris." Cosette waved at the room with a shrug. "Mamie was too ill to travel, and Jean wouldn't leave her behind." She stared at Haley. "And I wouldn't leave Jean behind."

Haley found she was holding her breath. It was obvious by the darkness in Cosette's eyes that the memories she was recalling were tragic. "What happened?" Haley asked softly.

"Jean's reputation as an excellent chef was renowned in the town, and it wasn't long before the Boche heard about him. I'll never forget the cold winter night near the end of 1917 when they pounded on our door and demanded Jean run the kitchen for an important New Year's Eve party. I, stupidly, was too frightened to hide, and when they saw me, they insisted I come too. Jean was livid, but we didn't dare protest."

Cosette paused her story to sip her coffee, then continued. "Jean was so nervous and angry. Angry that our mother had died, angry that our father had left us in Rethal, angry that our mamie was dying and that the Boche were forcing us to leave her alone so we could serve them at their party. Angry that they'd entered France and claimed it as their own."

"I take it the party didn't go well," Haley said.

"No. An English spy was recognised. Stupid girl. The commander took it out on all of us who worked there, especially, for some reason, my brother." She pointed to the scar on her cheek. "And me. This happened there." Cosette smiled mirthlessly. "I think this is why I recognised your friend, and she didn't recognise me."

"Mrs. Reed was there?"

"Of course." Cosette laughed. "You should see your face. You didn't know your friend was a spy?"

Haley had had her suspicions, but Ginger could be very evasive when she wanted to be and was resolutely silent whenever the topic presented itself. Haley would keep the confirmation to herself. She'd wait for Ginger to tell her if she wanted to, but Haley doubted Ginger would ever break her vow to the Crown. Not if she could help it.

Cosette sneered. "It's Madame Reed's fault that Jean died that night."

Haley would argue that it was the fault of the Boche, but she didn't think it wise to say so at that moment.

Cosette continued, "A couple of months later, our grandmother died. I stayed in her house until after the war since I couldn't get back to Paris before then."

"I'm sorry for your loss," Haley said. "I lost my brother to a violent death."

"Everyone lost someone during the war," Cosette snapped. "You're not unique."

Haley stayed quiet. Cosette wasn't in the frame of mind to be comforted.

"My father had lived here in this flat that whole time, can you imagine? Living the life while Jean, mamie, and I suffered." Cosette shot Haley a look. "He didn't last long once I got home." Snorting, she added, "Arsenic. A few drops onto his food every day."

"You killed him?" Haley asked, incredulous. Though it was hardly surprising, in retrospect, that Sabine Chapdelaine hadn't been Cosette's first kill.

"He abandoned us to the Boche!" Cosette said. "I enjoyed watching him gradually become ill and not knowing what was wrong." Cosette glanced away. "He died in debt, living extravagantly while other men sacrificed and fought. It meant there was no money to pay for university for me to become a scientist. I was destined to be nothing more than a lowly maid, doing several jobs day and night, seven days a week. Even though I have this flat, I can't afford the bills, taxes, and upkeep."

"Would he not have provided for you?" Haley asked, "If . . . he hadn't died?"

Cosette picked up a box of matches from near the candle on the table. "He was too lazy. It would've been me providing for him." She struck a match and lit it.

The flickering candle caught Haley's attention.

It had a flat, fruity smell, not sweet, but not exactly the honey scent of beeswax.

Cosette looked shiftily over the rim of her teacup. "Are you certain your friend is even called Ginger Reed? Just how well do you know her?"

"Well enough," Haley said. "We met a couple of times during the war but didn't become friends again until we found each other in Boston."

"America," Cosette said dreamily. "It's my one regret. Not getting to see the shores of the new world.

"There's time yet," Haley said.

"I think we both know there's no time left for me."

"Why would you say that?" Haley held a hand to her stomach, which rolled suddenly with a shot of pain. When was the last time she'd eaten?

"Where is Madame Reed?" Cosette asked. "Why isn't she here with you? I heard she was released from the hospital, though she didn't come back to the villa last night."

A ribbon of alarm coursed through Haley's heart. Cosette was still on the hunt for Ginger. Cosette blamed her for her brother's demise. "She's gone back to London."

"Oh." The small word escaped Cosette's mouth. Her eyes flashed with disappointment. "I see."

"Did you poison them, Cosette?" Haley asked. "Was it you?"

Cosette lifted a shoulder. "It's only a matter of time before they find me," she said without fully admitting her guilt. "*You* found me." Grabbing at her stomach, she winced, then added, "I've only the guillotine to look forward to."

Haley felt light-headed. She stared at her cup with confusion. It was still full of coffee, now grown cold. With alarm, she watched as Cosette's chin fell to her chest, almost as if she'd fallen asleep at the table.

"Cosette. Cosette!"

Haley's words came out thickly. Her mind raced to make sense of things. They were being poisoned, but how?

Her gaze landed on the candle, its flame flickering ominously.

As if swimming through rapids, Haley raised an arm and slapped out the candle, just as she fell into blackness.

23

Ginger raced outside, waved down the nearest taxicab, and climbed into the backseat. Her mind was so fixed on Haley and the potential danger she might be in that she was caught off guard when the backseat door on the other side of the vehicle opened.

"It's taken!" she shouted.

Her protestation didn't stop the man from sliding in and grinning.

"Louis!"

Louis tipped his hat. "You don't mind if we share the fare, do you?"

"What are you doing here?" Ginger scowled. "Are you following me?"

"If you're asking if I have reason to be concerned

about your welfare, then, *oui*."

The taxi driver stared back at Ginger through the rear-view mirror. "Madame?"

Ginger, annoyed that she couldn't get Louis out of her taxicab without making a scene, or worse, further injuring the former agent's leg, gave the driver Cosette Padou's address.

Louis gave her a short nod. "Where I expected you would be going."

Ginger narrowed her gaze. Did he know? Testing him, she asked, "Where?"

"Mademoiselle Padou's place, *naturellement*."

Ginger wasn't surprised by Louis' astuteness. He had to be of a certain intelligence to have qualified for recruitment to wartime assignments.

"You are concerned about your friend?" Louis continued, "Mademoiselle Higgins."

Returning a sharp glance, Ginger asked, "Why do you presume that?"

"Because you exited her building like a dog was nipping at your heels." He inclined his head. "Up to now, the two of you have been working on the case together."

Ginger worked her lips. Louis was an excellent spy and better as a friend than an enemy. She softened her look. "I am, in fact, a little concerned. If I'm correct in deducing that Mademoiselle Padou is our poisoner, Miss Higgins could be in trouble."

Louis frowned "Hopefully, soon, we can relieve your fears, Madame Reed."

Ginger could only nod in agreement. Before too long, the driver came to a stop. Ginger had the coins in her hand in anticipation and beat Louis' delayed offer to pay. It was a glimpse into how Louis might've operated with Mme Chapdelaine, the lady with money, and the gentleman who pretended to belong to her class.

In a typical situation, Ginger would politely wait for Louis to join her before heading inside, but his bad leg made his exit from the taxicab cumbersome . . . and then there were the stairs. She simply couldn't loiter.

Brass postal cubbyholes lined the wall on one side of the entrance, which was papered in green stripes and had a well-worn black-and-white checked floor. A wooden staircase curled up on the opposite side, and Ginger raced up the steps. Once on the correct floor, Ginger found Cosette's flat; she knocked firmly while speaking loudly, "Cosette? Haley?"

No footsteps. No voices. No sound. Only the uneven clomp of Louis pulling himself up the stairs.

"Cosette?" Ginger tried the door handle and found it unlocked. Surely the inhabitants of this flat would lock the door when they left? Paris wasn't exactly a low-crime city.

Greeted with a strange odour, Ginger immediately covered her nose and mouth with a gloved hand. She took the first door, which opened to a small kitchen, and her heart froze. Cosette and Haley's bodies were lying partially on the table as if they'd suddenly needed a nap.

"Haley!"

Though Ginger's first instinct was to help her friend, she hurried to the closed window and heaved it open, letting the fresh air fill the room. Luckily, a foot officer was in view, and Ginger waved her arms frantically, calling out in French that two women were in distress and needed a doctor, *tout de suite*!

Louis reached the flat just as Ginger pulled Haley onto her back on the floor.

"In the kitchen," Ginger said, knowing Louis would find her by following her voice. "I think they've been poisoned."

"Are they breathing?" Louis said, finding them.

Ginger lowered her ear to Haley's mouth. "Miss Higgins is." Ginger placed two fingers on Haley's neck, checking her pulse. "It's weak but there."

Louis placed two fingers on Cosette's neck, and Ginger stared back with a questioning look.

He nodded. "She's still alive." He pulled Cosette onto her back beside Haley.

In what seemed like an interminable amount of time, a doctor arrived, a haggard-looking man with black, oiled-back hair. Ginger explained in French she thought the women might have been poisoned.

"*Avec quoi?*" With what?

Cosette had used two poisons already: chloroform and cyanide. "I don't know," she said. "But we should have the coffee tested."

Haley moaned, and Ginger's heart leaped with relief. Her friend wasn't out of the woods, but she was alive and reviving.

"Haley, it's me, Ginger. You're going to be all right."

"Candle," she muttered.

Ginger remembered the strange burning smell that had accosted her when she'd stepped inside. "Of course. We'll be sure to test the candle. Now you just rest. An ambulance is on its way."

24

It was Ginger's turn to visit Haley in hospital. Her curly, untamed hair seemed to take over her pillow. Although her breathing was stable, it was raspy as the poison had been inhaled. She'd burned her right hand when she used it to extinguish the candle, and it had been cleaned and wrapped up by an efficient nurse.

"I'm fine," Haley insisted.

"We'll wait until the doctors agree," Ginger said, smiling.

Haley continued with her argument. "But I'm a *nurse*. I can tend to myself."

Ginger huffed. "I've got no doubt about it."

"I could just leave like you did," Haley huffed. "Sneak down the stairwell."

"The difference, *ma chérie*, was that we didn't know who had tried to kill me at the time. We know who tried to kill you, and she's been apprehended. Your life is no longer in danger. At least not from her."

It'd been two days since Ginger and Louis had rescued Haley and Cosette before the poisoning had done its job. Like Haley, Cosette was conscious, though weak. Despite her raw vocal cords, she had confessed her misdeeds to Inspector Tremblay.

Ginger snorted as she imagined that conversation. The inspector had been so certain that Mr. Miller was his man. If it hadn't been for Ginger and Haley's investigative work, an innocent man would've been convicted of murder.

Cosette had admitted to her part in Mme Chapdelaine's death, though she insisted it was an accident. On the day of the garden party, she'd given Denis Faucher from La Petite Porte Rouge a little arsenic, enough to make him ill. She believed she'd have greater control of how the drinks were made and who received them if he wasn't present. Taking a blue glass had been a last-minute, impulsive decision. Cosette reasoned it would help her know which glass had the poison in it, presumably so the desired person would get the drink. Unfortunately, it hadn't worked since the poisonous drink had been intended for Ginger. When Inspector Tremblay had recited the confession, he quoted Cosette, "Elise, that simpleton, couldn't get one simple instruction right!" Except, it turned out, to return the blue glass to La Petite Porte Rouge. Elise, on further interrogation, had insisted she meant to give the drink to Ginger, but Mme Chapdelaine had intercepted her and swooped the blue glass off the tray.

Cosette's second attempt at killing Ginger was at the fashion parade, and if it hadn't been for Haley's quick thinking, she might've succeeded.

Inspector Tremblay's eyes shone with intrigue when he repeated Cosette's motive. "She thinks you're responsible for her brother's death! Proof that her mind is gone. M. Padou died at the hands of the Boche in occupied territory. How could you have been involved with that, ha, ha?"

Ginger had done her best to look profoundly bewildered, but her heart was sickened. The war was still taking lives nine years after it had ended.

A knocking at the door of the shared hospital room produced Dr. Lyon. "Mademoiselle. 'Iggins! I am so pleased you are alive!"

Ginger smiled, first at the jovial doctor, then at Haley, who couldn't keep from flashing a broad grin.

"I am too," Haley said. "Do you have news?"

"Indeed, I do." Dr. Lyon's eyes grew round with excitement. "Quite ingenious, rather, if not nefarious."

"How did she do it?" Ginger asked.

"Oleander!"

Ginger knew enough about the tree to know the wood, leaves, and blossoms were deadly.

"She concentrated the glycoside," Haley said.

"Yes!" the doctor agreed. "Then soaked the wick in it. The smoke from burning it would be toxic and potentially lethal in a confined space if burned long enough."

"Cosette's kitchen was small, and she had the door and window closed," Ginger said. "But why would she do it? Her resentment was directed at me."

"She may have thought she'd hurt you more if she went after someone you cared for," Dr. Lyon said.

"I told her you'd gone back to England," Haley said. "She seemed to know that she was going to be caught. She was without money and family. An exit of this sort might've been part of her plan. It would explain the existence of the candle."

"What's going to happen to Mademoiselle Padou

now?" Ginger asked. In London, the girl would face a noose, though many women managed to be sent to an asylum for the criminally insane instead.

"I'm afraid the guillotine is in her future," Dr. Lyon said. "It's barbaric but quick and painless."

Oh mercy.

GINGER REMAINED in Paris for an extra week to ensure Haley was on her feet again once she was released from hospital.

"I can't stay away from my family any longer," Ginger explained. Basil had been understanding, even though he had made no bones about his concern for Ginger's welfare and that the children were missing her dearly.

"Of course," Haley said. "You've stayed too long. I'm returning to my studies tomorrow. I have a lot to catch up on now. You'll let me see you to the train station?"

"So long as you promise it won't be the last time I see you," Ginger said. "My offer for you to spend the winter holidays with us in London still stands."

"Beats facing the rocky seas to go back to Boston," Haley said with a grin. "I'll take you up on it."

. . .

After a long day of travel the next day, Ginger was finally in the comfort of her own home and in the arms of her loving husband, cosying together in the sitting room. The curtains at the tall south-facing windows were drawn, a fire burned cheerfully in the large stone fireplace, flickering light onto *The Mermaid* painting above the mantel, and Boss was curled up in his bed near the hearth.

"I don't think I can ever let you out of my sight again," Basil said, his voice a mix of seriousness and jest. "You seem to attract trouble wherever you go."

"I'm sure that's not entirely fair," Ginger said. She raised her glass of brandy in the air. "But all's well that ends well."

"I never did care for that sentiment." After a sigh, Basil added, "You're home now, and it's a good thing. You are the hub of the wheel here, Ginger, and things were wobbling out of order at a concerning speed."

Ginger laughed. "What do you mean? Everyone is safe and healthy." Mrs. Beasley was still cooking delicious meals, Pippins continued to amaze her with his vitality at his advanced years, Nanny Green and Lizzie had arrived with Rosa, all in good health and spirits, and things were functioning in the house and in the nursery as if Ginger hadn't been away. Scout was eager to return to his equestrian school and even admitted to enjoying his time in Paris. Felicia and Charles were still in love, and though Felicia had been directed by her doctor to rest in bed, she was still with child. Ambrosia, despite growing frailty, was as headstrong as ever. She'd slowed down over the years, but her wit was as keen as ever.

"People tend to drop like flies around you, Ginger," she'd said during the evening meal. "Perhaps it's time to change your perfume."

Basil pulled Ginger to his side, and she leaned in under his arm. "I suppose it's me who wobbles when you're gone, love. You're the hub of my wheel."

Ginger tilted her head up and kissed her husband's warm lips. She really couldn't imagine her life without him or anyone else in her family now. "And you are mine."

Boss pushed himself onto his haunches, his big brown eyes staring at Ginger and Basil. After a quick scratch behind his ear, he sauntered over to the settee. Ginger patted the spot beside her. "Come and join us, Bossy."

Boss jumped up, nudged Ginger's arm with his wet nose, and curled into a ball.

Ginger sighed with contentment. She had so much to be thankful for. Hartigan House and everyone in it was a blessing and a gift. She turned to Basil.

"Have you heard how Marvin is doing?"

Marvin Elliot, Scout's cousin, had been injured in a shooting incident and had been left in a compromised state, both mentally and physically.

"He's improved," Basil said, "but . . ."

"He can't care for himself properly," Ginger interjected. "I think he should come and live with us."

Basil raised a brow. "Won't that be rather . . . awkward?"

Ginger knew what Basil meant. Scout was the "young master" of Hartigan House, and Marvin could be nothing more than a servant.

"He'll end up a beggar on the streets," Ginger said. "We can't let that happen."

"You're right," Basil said. "Though it will take the household time to get used to him."

"So, you'll arrange it?" Ginger asked.

"I will."

Ginger stretched out her arms, feeling ready for bed. "I'm going to the nursery to see Rosa before turning in," she said.

Basil stretched his legs in front of him. "I'll be right behind you."

Before Ginger reached the door, Pippins stepped inside. His shoulders seemed to have curled in even more since she'd last seen him, diminishing his height. The electric light shone off his bald head, but his eyes, growing smaller behind sagging skin, remained the bright cornflower blue she remembered as a child.

"Pips?" Ginger started. "Is everything all right."

"Yes, madam. I had word from a former employer. She'd like me to come for a visit, and I was wondering if it would be all right with you."

Ginger blinked back her surprise. Pippins had been with her family since she was a little girl, except for the ten years when her father had taken them to America. During that time, George Hartigan had lent their butler to a distant cousin whom Ginger had yet to meet.

"Do you mean Florence Hartigan?"

"Yes, madam."

The request was highly unusual. Florence Hartigan had to be rather long in the tooth and Ginger felt a twinge of guilt at not having contacted her before.

The question remained: what did she want from

Pippins? One didn't usually call on a former butler out of the blue without reason.

"Of course you may go, Pippins. But do you think you'll be all right to travel? I've just returned from doing a fair bit, and I found it rather rigorous."

"I think I can manage sitting on a train for a couple of hours, madam, but I do appreciate your concern."

"When will you go?"

"Next week."

"Very well. It'll give me time to write a letter. Perhaps she'll come to London one day. I would truly like to meet her."

"I shall enquire on your behalf, madam." He bowed, then retreated.

Ginger turned back to Basil. "How very odd indeed."

"You've never mentioned a cousin," he said.

"Honestly, I'd quite forgotten I had one."

As Ginger stepped along the marble floors of the entrance hall and up the plush green carpet runner on the staircase, her mind pondered this familial lapse. Perhaps over the holidays, she'd rectify things. Haley would return, and it would be the first Christmas with little Rosa.

Ginger couldn't wait.

Don't miss the next Ginger Gold mystery~
MURDER AT YULETIDE

Have Yourself a Merry Little Murder

Clive Pippins, Lady Ginger Gold's beloved, elderly butler is Christmas shopping when a body is found. To the shock of everyone in Ginger's household, the victim is the spinster cousin Pippins worked for during the years surrounding the Great War.

As Ginger and her good friend Haley Higgins investigate, things begin to look grim for Ginger's dear butler. What had the man been up to during the war years, and had he been complicit in a crime?

What secret was Pips holding onto?

And worse, would he go down for murder by refusing to divulge it?

The only gift Ginger wants for the Christmas of 1927 is for her butler to be exonerated in time to ring in the new year!

Buy on AMAZON or read Free with Kindle Unlimited!

———

ACKNOWLEDGMENTS

I know I don't acknowledge them enough, but this book wouldn't be what it is without the sharp eyes and skilled edits of **Angelika Offenwanger** (who enhanced the Paris setting), **Robbi Bryant**, and **Heather Belleguelle** who "put her French degree to good use."

Thank you, ladies. You make the journey so much easier!

Sign up for Lee's readers list and gain access to **Ginger Gold's private Journal.** Find out about Ginger's Life before the SS *Rosa* and how she became the woman she has. This is a fluid document that will cover her romance with her late husband Daniel, her time serving in the British secret service during World War One, and beyond. Includes a recipe for Dark Dutch Chocolate Cake!

It begins: **July 31, 1912**

How fabulous that I found this Journal today, hidden in the bottom of my wardrobe. Good old Pippins, our English butler in London, gave it to me as a parting gift when Father whisked me away on our American adventure so he could marry Sally. Pips said it was for me to record my new adventures. I'm ashamed I never even penned one word before today. I think I was just too sad.

This old leather-bound journal takes me back to that emotional time. I had shed enough tears to fill the ocean and I remember telling

Father dramatically that I was certain to cause flooding to match God's. At eight years old I was well-trained in my biblical studies, though, in retro-spect, I would say that I had probably bordered on heresy with my little tantrum.

The first week of my "adventure" was spent with a tummy ache and a number of embarrassing sessions that involved a bucket and Father holding back my long hair so I wouldn't soil it with vomit.

I certainly felt that I was being punished for some reason. Hartigan House—though large and sometimes lonely—was my home and Pips was my good friend. He often helped me to pass the time with games of I Spy and Xs and Os.

"Very good, Little Miss," he'd say with a twinkle in his blue eyes when I won, which I did often. I suspect now that our good butler wasn't beyond letting me win even when unmerited.

Father had got it into his silly head that I needed a mother, but I think the truth was he wanted a wife. Sally, a woman half my father's age, turned out to be a sufficient wife in the end, but I could never claim her as a mother.

Well, Pips, I'm sure you'd be happy to know that things turned out all right here in America.

SUBSCRIBE to read more!

•

Murder by Plum Pudding

Murder on Fleet Street

Murder at Brighton Beach

Murder in Hyde Park

Murder at the Royal Albert Hall

Murder in Belgravia

Murder on Mallowan Court

Murder at the Savoy

Murder at the Circus

Murder in France

Murder at Yuletide

LADY GOLD INVESTIGATES (Ginger Gold companion short stories)

Volume 1

Volume 2

Volume 3

Volume 4

HIGGINS & HAWKE MYSTERY SERIES (cozy 1930s historical)

The 1930s meets Rizzoli & Isles in this friendship depression era cozy mystery series.

Death at the Tavern

Death on the Tower

Death on Hanover

Death by Dancing

THE ROSA REED MYSTERIES

(1950s cozy historical)

Murder at High Tide

Murder on the Boardwalk

Murder at the Bomb Shelter

Murder on Location

Murder and Rock 'n Roll

Murder at the Races

Murder at the Dude Ranch

Murder in London

Murder at the Fiesta

Murder at the Weddings

**A NURSERY RHYME MYSTERY
SERIES (mystery / sci fi)**

*Marlow finds himself teamed up with intelligent and savvy
Sage Farrell, a girl so far out of his league he feels blinded in*

her presence - literally - damned glasses! Together they work to find the identity of @gingerbreadman. Can they stop the killer before he strikes again?

Gingerbread Man

Life Is but a Dream

Hickory Dickory Dock

Twinkle Little Star

LIGHT & LOVE (sweet romance)

Set in the dazzling charm of Europe, follow Katja, Gabriella, Eva, Anna and Belle as they find strength, hope and love.

Love Song

Your Love is Sweet

In Light of Us

Lying in Starlight

PLAYING WITH MATCHES (WW2 history/romance)

A sobering but hopeful journey about how one young German boy copes with the war and propaganda. Based on true events.

A Piece of Blue String (companion short story)

THE CLOCKWISE COLLECTION (YA time travel romance)

Casey Donovan has issues: hair, height and uncontrollable trips to the 19th century! And now this ~ she's accidentally taken Nate Mackenzie, the cutest boy in the school, back in time. Awkward.

Clockwise

Clockwiser

Like Clockwork

Counter Clockwise

Clockwork Crazy

Clocked (companion novella)

Standalones

Seaweed

Love, Tink

ABOUT THE AUTHOR

Lee Strauss is a USA TODAY bestselling author of The Ginger Gold Mysteries series, The Higgins & Hawke Mystery series, The Rosa Reed Mystery series (cozy historical mysteries), A Nursery Rhyme Mystery series (mystery suspense), The Light & Love series (sweet romance), The Clockwise Collection (YA time travel romance), and young adult historical fiction with over a million books read. She has titles published in German and French, and a growing audio library.

When Lee's not writing or reading she likes to cycle, hike, and stare at the ocean. She loves to drink caffè lattes and red wines in exotic places, and eat dark chocolate anywhere.

For more info on books by Lee Strauss and her social media links, visit leestraussbooks.com. To make sure you don't miss the next new release, be sure to sign up for her readers' list!

Discuss the books, ask questions, share your

opinions. Fun giveaways! Join the Lee Strauss Readers' Group on Facebook for more info.

Did you know you can follow your favourite authors on Bookbub? If you subscribe to Bookbub — (and if you don't, why don't you? - They'll send you daily emails alerting you to sales and new releases on just the kind of books you like to read!) — follow me to make sure you don't miss the next Ginger Gold Mystery!

www.leestraussbooks.com
leestraussbooks@gmail.com